I0891397

CONCHO VALLEY

Center Point
Large Print

Also by Barry Cord and available from Center Point Large Print:

The Long Wire
Dry Range
The Iron Trail Killers
Trouble in Peaceful Valley
Boss of Barbed Wire

This Large Print Book carries the Seal of Approval of N.A.V.H.

CONCHO VALLEY

BARRY CORD

Center Point Large Print
Thorndike, Maine

This Center Point Large Print edition
is published in the year 2024 by arrangement with
Golden West Inc.

Copyright © 1958 by Arcadia House.
Copyright © renewed 1986 by Arcadia House.

All rights reserved.

Originally published in the US by Arcadia House.
Originally published in the UK by Frederick Muller.

The text of this Large Print edition is unabridged.
In other aspects, this book may vary
from the original edition.
Printed in the United States of America
on permanent paper sourced using
environmentally responsible foresting methods.
Set in 16-point Times New Roman type.

ISBN 979-8-89164-005-4 (hardcover)
ISBN 979-8-89164-009-2 (paperback)

The Library of Congress has cataloged this record
under Library of Congress Control Number: 2023946255

CONCHO VALLEY

CHAPTER I

The gusty wind whipped sand over the two workmen lowering the pine coffin into the hole. They braced themselves against it, cursing silently. Behind them the wagon horses blew noisily, jangling bit irons in their uneasy restlessness.

The woman stood at the head of the second grave, beside the tall, bony minister reading from his Bible. She stood with bowed head, black dress whipping against her legs; she held a crumpled white handkerchief to her face and listened with remote ear to the Reverend's droning.

There was no one at Luke's funeral, as there had been no one at their wedding. She stood braced against the wind, her eyes closed; she seemed to be listening to another voice, a long way from Concho Valley, asking in happier vein:

"Do you, Louella Pringle, take this man for your lawful wedded husband?"

Had it been only six months ago?

She had been fair with Luke. She had married him in Cheyenne. She did not love him; she had scarcely known him. But she was tired of supporting her shiftless father, tired of working as a waitress in a noisy frontier lunchroom, and

Luke, in town with a Diamond T trail drive, was the only man who had asked her.

"I tried, Luke," she whispered now. There was an aching regret in her now that he'd never know. "I really tried."

He had taken her on her terms. He was a patient man, he had told her, and he loved her. A strange man, with a hidden streak of sentiment; a shy man who stood apart from his rough trail mates. The kind of man who would name his small spread Rainbow, and with smiling seriousness tell her she was the treasure every man sought at the end of his personal rainbow. . . .

In time she might have come to love him. But there was no more time. Time had ended abruptly yesterday morning, when they had driven into Rainbow's yard and callously dumped the bodies in front of her door.

She had been in the bedroom, fallen into a fitful, exhausted sleep after a long night of waiting. She came to the door and stumbled over Luke's body.

"We caught them rustling our beef, Mrs. Snow!" Charley Mizner, Diamond T's foreman, was in the wagon seat. A half-dozen riders were grouped around him.

"You know Miss Telfors' orders. . . ."

Louella sank to her knees beside Luke, too shocked and tired to think clearly. That was all Charley Mizner had said, all the explanation he had had for the wife of the man he had hanged.

Luke's coffin grated now on the bottom of the grave, and the man nearest her pulled the rope sling free. He coiled it and stowed it under the wagon seat and, turning, glanced upward in quick apprehension. His companion, leaning on the handle of his shovel, followed his involuntary appraisal.

They made a harsh backdrop to this lonely, tearless funeral, those riders on the rim of Sentinel Butte. They stood out clearly above the dust storm raging across the valley below; they were not more than a half-mile from Concho's small cemetery and plainly visible.

There were a round dozen of them, surveying the scene in ominous silence. It was Diamond T's way of expressing its contempt for Concho, and a warning to any who might be tempted to take sides.

Reverend Stone kept his head down, his eyes on the passage he was reading. His voice rose above the wind. ". . . *And to dust thou returnest* . . ." And then it was over. He stooped to pick up a handful of sand and tossed it over Luke Snow's remains.

Louella Snow did not move. The minister took her arm. He was a tall, lean man with gaunt, Lincolnesque features. His blue eyes held an angry sorrow.

"There's nothing more we can do for them,

Louella," he said gently. "Let me take you home. Amy will have tea—"

Luke's widow raised her eyes to the silent watchers on the rim, and a deep hate tore through the empty shield of her grief.

"You're wrong, Reverend! There is something I can do for Luke—and for the man we buried with him. I'm staying on at Rainbow. And some day I'll make Nina Telfors pay for the hanging of my husband!"

Lou Winters came into Concho Valley by way of the old Comanche Wash trail. Coming out of this narrow sandstone canyon, he caught the brunt of the sandstorm sweeping across the valley.

His roan snorted and backed around, shaking his head and blowing. Winters tugged his faded red bandana up to cover his mouth and nose and jammed his gray cavalryman's hat down over his eyes.

Sentinel Butte was directly across the narrow neck of the valley, but he did not know it. The dust storm cut visibility to a few yards. He rode slowly until he met a wider and more deeply rutted road curving away from the sandstone bluffs at his back.

He hazarded a guess and turned right, riding with the wind almost directly behind him.

Fifteen minutes later he saw the first shack

loom up and relaxed, knowing that the town of Concho must be just ahead.

The roan snorted and danced off the trail as a tumbleweed came rolling up from behind. Lou put his glance on the cabin and found it to be an abandoned dwelling, sagging forlornly.

Someone had used it lately as a billboard. The two posters newly tacked to the roadside wall caught his attention, and he pulled the roan in close, eyeing them through slitted lids.

REWARD

$1,000 $1,000

One thousand dollars will be paid for apprehension or information leading to apprehension of ACE DOOLIN or any member of his gang.

N. Telfors.

The other poster read:

NOTICE

All strangers caught on Diamond T land will be promptly hanged.

By order of N. Telfors.

Lou settled back in the saddle, a bleak smile twisting his lips. "Pretty high-handed cuss, this N. Telfors," he observed dryly. "Or else a jittery one."

He was a rangy, easy-moving man, not inclined to humor. Three years of war, a sabre slash across his right thigh and a shrapnel scar under his left ear had squeezed the lightness from him. He was a man who had taken orders and given them; he had accepted this as a condition of war. But he was not the sort to take lightly what he considered an infringement on his freedom of movement, and the blunt notice roused a rebellious streak in him.

He wondered how his partner, Frank Santree, had taken this arrogant notice, and uneasiness tightened his mouth.

Frank had come to Concho Valley four days ago, while Lou had ridden on to the Mexican border on business. Frank had wanted to look up an old friend, Luke Snow—he had promised to join Lou in Salinas, a day's ride from Concho Valley.

But Frank was overdue, and Lou had come to see what was detaining him. . . .

The wind tore at the posters, making them vibrate against the weathered boards. Lou swung the roan back onto the road. He crested the small rise leading to town in time to pull up sharply as a buggy, coming down the hill on his right, cut in front of him.

A long-shanked, bony man, obviously a preacher, was driving. The woman on the seat beside him was young enough to outshine the drab black dress she wore and the cold immobility of her face. Her glance touched him and went through him; she looked past him with remote interest.

Reverend Stone gave Winters a longer scrutiny. Then the buggy was whirring away and Lou saw only their stiff backs through the murk. He touched heels to the roan's dust-caked flanks and followed.

The town of Concho opened up, and he was mildly surprised to find the settlement bigger than he had expected. This was high semi-desert country, off the main stage road, and even in Salinas few people had ever heard of Concho.

A double row of false-fronted structures, many of them yellow-brown adobe, flanked the wide street known as Lee Avenue. Three buildings poked their roofs above the rest of the building line. The first and nearest was the stone bank on the corner. The second was the hotel, two blocks down. And at the far end of town, forming a backdrop, rose the thin white-painted spire of a New England–style church.

The dust storm was keeping most people indoors. Except for the wagon pulled up before the general store, Lou saw no other sign of life on the wide street. The walks were deserted and some of the shops had boarded their windows.

Lou eased his roan to the south side of the street and watched the buggy make a turn at the third corner. Broken by the buildings around him, the force of the windstorm was less intense here; he eased back in the saddle and thumbed his hat up from his eyes.

He had no idea where Frank Santree might be, except that he would be with Luke Snow, quite possibly on some small spread in the valley. He was not likely to be in town on a day like this, Lou speculated.

But he had to start somewhere. His questing glance caught the sign above the door just ahead: TOM'S BAR. He tied up at the empty rack and went inside.

The place was dead. A sour-faced man with thin brown hair plastered across his bald spot was dunking dirty glasses in a bucket of soapy water. He looked up as Lou entered, frowned slightly, and began drying his red hands on his apron.

There was a drunk sleeping with his head down on the table in a corner of the room; his snoring rasped unevenly in the empty room.

Lou walked to the bar. He took a look around, and when the bartender moved up to him Lou asked: "Town always quiet like this on a Wednesday afternoon?"

The bartender shrugged. "Only when we have a funeral."

"Someone important?"

"Depends." The man's voice held a wary neutrality. "From the Diamond T's point of view, they wasn't. Just another couple of rustlers they caught red-handed and strung up."

"Diamond T's real rough on rustlers, eh?" Lou mused, thinking of the poster he had read.

"Rough on Luke Snow's widder, too," the bartender muttered. He broke off as two men came stamping into the bar.

Lou turned and looked them over. Range-clad, dusty men with bandanas covering their nose. They pulled the bandanas down as they came toward the bar, brushed sand from their clothes.

Both men wore six-shooters in thonged-down holsters—gunfighter style!

They came up to the bar and looked Lou over. The man nearest Winters was dark, wiry, restless. He reminded Lou a little of his partner. Frank had been driven by an inner restlessness, an itch to keep moving, to push, probe, challenge. It had gotten Santree in a lot of trouble. . . .

The man behind was tall and sandy-haired; he had an innocent, boyish face, though he was at least thirty.

"Just got time for a quick one, Tom," the wiry gunster said. He had a quick, demanding voice. His mouth twisted in a sneer. "Didn't see many town folk at the funeral—"

Tom Sands placed glasses in front of them and reached behind him for a bottle. His movements were slow and careful.

"Thought Will Baxter would be out there," the

gunman persisted. "Hear he's been making a lot of threats against Diamond T lately."

Tom shrugged. "I wouldn't know, Keeler. I mind my own business. I've got nothing against Diamond T."

Lou was frowning, an improbable thought nagging him.

"You say the funeral was for Luke Snow?" He put his words to the bartender. "Luke and who else?"

Tom's hand jerked; he spilled whiskey and cursed softly as he reached for a sopping cloth.

Keeler turned. He looked Lou over again, judging the rangy man with new interest.

"Reckon I can help you, fella." His voice held suspicion and a rising challenge. "The brush-popper we caught riding with Luke Snow called himself Frank Santree. I helped string him up!"

Lou put the palm of his left hand over his glass and slowly pushed it away from him. A dismal feeling dampened the cold shock of the gunman's revelation. He measured the two of them, and he had a moment's bitter wonder at what Frank Santree had gotten himself into.

"This Frank—he a friend of yores?" Keeler's voice held a probing edge. His companion had stepped back from the rail; he was facing Lou, his body slack.

"I knew him," Lou admitted. Temper fought against an old habit of discipline. He wanted no trouble until he knew what he was getting into. It looked to him as though Frank Santree had ridden into Concho Valley at the wrong time. Maybe Frank's friend, Luke, had been rustling Diamond T beef. Diamond T was a big ranch, and some men thought it fair game to steal from a spread that counted its beef in the thousands.

But he remembered the posters he had read on his way to town; one of them had puzzled him. There was more to this business than he could see at the moment.

He dropped a half-dollar on the bar to pay for his drink and turned to go. But the wiry man wasn't through with him.

He thrust out his foot, and Winters stumbled over it. He went down to his hands and knees, temper slashing through him. But he caught himself in time, the quick scraping of feet behind him warning him.

"So you knew Frank?" the man nagged. "Might be you was one of the lucky ones who got away. Could even be yo're one of Ace Doolin's riders, like yore friend was!"

Lou made no sudden move. The two men backed against the bar were just waiting for him to make a move they could interpret as hostile—and he would be dead before he could turn to face them.

"Ace Doolin would be mighty surprised to hear that!" he muttered. He was facing the door, and he gambled they would not shoot him in the back, not with Tom watching.

He started for the door.

He had the feeling they were weighing him with puzzled anger; indecision lay heavy in the room.

Lou was almost at the door when it opened. The newcomer didn't come into the bar. He rested his hands on the batwings, his quick, impatient stare gliding past Lou to the men at the rail.

"I expected to find you boozehounds here!" His voice was harsh, authoritative. "Pay up and get out! The boss's waiting for us at the fork—"

"Wait a minnit, Charley!" Keeler interrupted. His voice held a warning anger. "Looks like me an' Bowie just cornered ourselves a prize polecat! Claims to be a friend of Frank Santree, the rustler we caught with Luke stealin' Diamond T beef!"

Charley Mizner put his glance squarely on Lou now. A frown pulled his thick blond brows together. He was a heavy, powerful man in his late thirties who dressed like a bank president, preferred driving a buggy to riding a horse. He was Diamond T's foreman, and some claimed he was its boss. Charley had ten armed men on his payroll and felt that was enough armament for Diamond T—he himself never wore a gun.

"That so?" he said. He had a pleasant voice; it might have sounded so in contrast to Keeler's rasping one.

Lou made a cold gesture. “I never knew it to be a crime until now,” he answered. He took a stride toward the door, but Charley stood solidly, smiling coldly, blocking his exit.

“Let’s take him back to the ranch for trial,” Keeler suggested. “Might be we have another noose to fill—”

Lou knew then that Keeler would not let him go. Diamond T obviously had a reputation for passing its own judgments and meting out its own punishments—and Lou didn’t figure to face a stacked jury.

Charley was directly in front of him, and Lou gambled that the two Diamond T men would not risk a shot now. He reached up in a swift lunge, hooked his fingers in Charley’s collar and hauled him into the room. Spinning him around, he shoved Charley toward the bar.

The Diamond T foreman stumbled and fell, sliding his hands through the sawdust around the rail. Keeler, spinning away to avoid him, lifted his Colt clear and fired once, last-minute eagerness spoiling his shot.

Lou’s return fire slammed him back against the bar. He twisted and stumbled over Charley and fell on him, rolling limply now.

Bowie, slower than Keeler, let his unfired Colt drop. He lifted his hands, his eyes bright with naked fear.

Charley heaved clear of Keeler’s body and

came to his feet. He looked at Keeler, then at Lou, and shook his head slowly. “You darn fool!” he muttered.

“Frank Santree was a friend of mine,” Lou said grimly. “But he didn’t ride for Doolin, and he wasn’t a rustler. Until four days ago Frank had never seen Concho Valley.” Lou sucked in a deep breath. “If Diamond T made a mistake, it’s a mistake it’s going to regret for the rest of its life. . . .”

Charley Mizner had recovered his poise. Ignoring the gun in Lou’s hand, he carefully straightened his rumpled clothing, dusted sawdust from his knees.

“Diamond T made no mistake!” he said coldly. “Luke Snow sold out to Ace Doolin. Frank was with Luke when we caught them.” He smiled crookedly. “Might be a case of your partner being caught with the wrong man at the wrong time. But with the trouble we’ve been having, we don’t have time to split hairs. If you’re Frank’s friend, get out of Concho Valley and keep riding. You won’t have another chance!”

“I’ll take the risk,” Lou snapped.

No one tried to stop him as he backed out. . . .

CHAPTER II

The Palms Hotel stood stolidly against the blustery wind sweeping down Lee Avenue. It was a two-story adobe structure reaching back from the street; it took up a whole block, as though whoever had erected it had felt the need of elbow room. An old adobe wall about six feet high, badly in need of repairs, circled it, and entrance to the hotel was through a wide gateway fronting on Lee Avenue.

It got its name, no doubt, from the two royal palms which flanked the entrance—a bizarre touch in this otherwise treeless town.

Lou Winters rode his roan between the palms, ducked as a dry frond tore loose and zigzagged down, and followed a path around the hotel to the stable in the back.

The wind kept up its sullen howling.

The big door was closed. He pushed it open and led the roan inside and waited until the hostler, a fat Mexican, showed up. The man took the roan, and Lou ducked out and crossed the yard to the hotel's side entrance and followed a narrow hallway into the lobby.

A chunky figure in store-bought clothes was at the desk, talking to the desk clerk, a tall, thin but pleasant-faced girl. He was wearing a cartridge belt and a holstered Colt, which didn't seem to go with the stiff cut of his cheap suit.

The girl was facing the lobby and she saw Lou come in; she made a slight warning gesture in his direction, and the chunky man turned and gave Lou a slow but not unfriendly stare.

Lou saw the star on his coat now and noticed that the lawman was young. He looked strong and compact and he had a square, stubborn jaw. But his eyes were blue and mild and somewhat uncertain as they measured Lou.

He nodded. "Howdy."

"Howdy yourself," Lou said, grinning. "Glad to hear a friendly voice, Sheriff."

"Town marshal," the other corrected. "Town policeman is a better fit. I'm George Asher."

"Lou Winters," Lou said, faintly amused. "Temporarily unemployed."

Asher dropped his gaze to the gun on Lou's hip. He read the man almost mechanically. *Left-handed gunslinger. Probably a new hand for Diamond T.*

He wanted to ask, but something in Lou's hard face stopped him. The wind flung sand against the lobby windows, and he said instead: "Not a good day to be travelling, mister."

Lou shrugged. He was reading the ink-stained register, looking for a clue that Frank Santree might have stopped there.

"A man's apt to get a wrong impression of

Concho," the marshal persisted. There was stiffness in his voice, and his neck held the flush of a stubborn, starting anger.

"Might," Lou said shortly. At the moment he did not wish to elaborate on the fact that it was more than the weather which had given him a bad impression of Concho.

He turned to the woman. She looked older from a distance; close up, he saw she was about the marshal's age. Her brown hair was caught up in an unsightly bun, and a lighter fuzz made sideburns on her pink cheeks.

"I'd like a room for a day or two. One with a lock."

The woman frowned. "All our rooms have locks," she said primly. "But if you have any valuables you're afraid of losing, I have a small safe here—"

"That's fine," Lou interrupted. He reached under his shirt and pulled out a money belt which he placed on the counter. She picked it up, and he said: "I'd like this to go with it, ma'am." He hauled a small chamois drawstring bag from his inner coat pocket, and she took both.

"I'll give you a receipt," she said.

He shrugged. "Reckon I don't need it, ma'am. The marshal looks like an honest man—"

Asher said bluntly: "And a curious one. You a cattle buyer?"

Lou shook his head. "Just passing through

town, Marshal." He picked up the quill pen and scratched his name on the register. The clerk was bent over the small iron safe, her back to Lou.

"No one just passes through Concho," the marshal said coldly. "It's way off the main trail. You got business here?"

"Could be," Lou murmured. He waited until the woman straightened, scratched out a receipt. "I'm looking for Ace Doolin."

Asher stiffened. A wary glint appeared in his blue eyes. "Doolin? The outlaw?"

Lou nodded. "Saw a poster just outside of town with his name on it, Marshal."

Asher shook his head. He seemed puzzled, and disappointed. "You won't find him in town," he muttered.

"You never can tell about Ace," Lou said dryly. He picked up his warbag and the key the woman handed him and turned toward the stairs.

Asher stepped away from the counter and followed him with hard eyes. Kathy Hastings, the desk clerk, said softly: "He one of them?"

Asher lifted his shoulders. "Could be. I'll see Will—"

Lou discovered that his square, beamed room overlooked a wide roofed veranda. The overhang deepened the early afternoon shadows in the room and cut some of the bluster of the wind. He walked to the casement window and pushed it open, and sand sifted across the worn Navajo rug by the oak-framed bed.

The world outside was a vast pall of dust. . . . He turned and sat on the bed, feeling grimy and tired. Behind the tiredness was a hollow feeling; Frank was dead, but it would take a little time to feel the shock of it.

There was a knock on the door and a Mexican boy came in, lugging a wooden bucket of water. Lou tossed the boy a two-bit piece and peeled off his shirt and underwear and splashed like a duck in a pond, drying himself finally on the towel by the washstand.

Refreshed, he sat on the bed again, a hard-muscled, bare-chested man strung a little taut over too many years. *Frank was dead!* Strung up by accident by a noose-hungry cattle outfit.

Or had it been an accident?

He shook his head. The story he had heard; the poster on the shack outside of town—it didn't make sense, in view of what he knew.

If Doolin was in Concho Valley, then the tip which had sent him to Salinas was all wrong. . . .

He pulled his discarded shirt toward him and reached for the tobacco sack and papers in his pocket; he made himself a cigaret with his thoughts on other things.

There had been three of them at the battle of Missionary Ridge. A man fought with a company and a regiment, and in the course of three bloody years he came to know a lot of men. Some died, some turned yellow, and some you never really knew, although you lived and worked with them twenty-four hours a day for months.

But he knew Frank Santree—and he thought he had known Ace Doolin. Only he hadn't been called Ace then, nor had it been Doolin. Herbert Dolan he'd been then—a man with a quick laugh, a devil-may-care attitude and a reputation as the best poker player in the regiment. Possibly that explained the "Ace." The Doolin might just have been some deputy sheriff's careless error. . . .

You'd lost track of the man after the war . . . and then something had come up and you'd looked for him almost two years—you and Frank. You'd looked for him because there had always been the three of you and it had become a habit. And now it had become important to find Doolin.

And then you found out that Herbert Dolan was Ace Doolin . . . and that he was hiding out in Mexico. . . .

Lou blew smoke out in a hard, violent gesture. He rose and walked to the window again, squinting across the dust pall, seeing nothing and not really wanting to see.

The story he had heard didn't make sense. Ace Doolin couldn't be in Concho Valley!

He finished his smoke and was pulling on a clean shirt when someone knocked on his door.

Lou called out and was tucking in his shirt tail

when the man entered. He came in with a quick, brusque air of impatience, closed the door and stood against it, an angry frown in his eyes.

"I'm Will Baxter!"

Lou finished tucking in his shirt, nodded civilly.

Baxter waited, as though expecting further comment. His voice held a rising note. "Didn't Knowles send you?"

Lou shook his head, smiled pleasantly. "I think you knocked on the wrong door, Baxter. Nobody sent me."

Will Baxter mopped his forehead. He was a slight man, who looked even thinner in the black broadcloth suit he wore. He had a narrow, not unhandsome face graced by a small black mustache and marred by a thin white scar which ran from just under his left ear to the point of his jaw. He looked angry and uncertain now.

"You said you were looking for Ace Doolin," he muttered.

Lou's eyes shadowed. "Reckon the marshal's been talking out of school." He walked over to the bed and made a motion to the one chair in the room. "Sit down, Baxter. Knowles didn't send me. I don't know who Knowles is. But if you know where Ace Doolin can be found, I'm interested."

Baxter hesitated. He made a small gesture compounded of weariness and disappointment.

"I don't know where Ace Doolin hangs out. That's the truth. According to Diamond T, he and his bunch have a hideout in the Tombstones."

"You don't believe Diamond T?"

"I hate Diamond T." Baxter's voice was soft, without emphasis. But it held an ugly note that gave a sharper impression of his feelings than any emphatic statement could have.

"Maybe we have that in common," Lou said levelly.

Baxter gave him a close look, then walked over to the chair. He took a couple of cigars from his vest pocket and extended one to Lou, who refused. Baxter leaned back and lighted up; he studied Lou through the smoke.

"What have you got against Diamond T?"

Lou smiled faintly. "I built up a resistance to orders during the war. . . ."

Baxter cocked his head to one side and then wagged it. "That isn't the whole reason, is it?"

"No." Lou leaned forward, the bed springs creaking under him. "Frank Santree was my partner!"

"Frank Santree?" Baxter's hands came together, his fingers steepling. Then he sat up straight in the chair. "Isn't that the man who was with Luke Snow? The man Charley Mizner claimed rode for Ace Doolin?"

Lou's lips pressed hard against his teeth. "I heard that's what Diamond T claimed," he admitted bleakly.

Baxter stood up. "I didn't know your partner.

I saw him when he came to town. I was in the lobby here, talking with Miss Hastings, when he stopped in, asked directions to Rainbow—"

"Rainbow?"

"Yes. Actually he asked where he could find Luke Snow—Rainbow is Luke's place." Baxter hunched forward, rolling his cigar between his lips. His eyes were moody. "I knew Luke pretty well. In a way, we both had worked for Diamond T—"

"I thought Luke had his own place here."

Baxter picked flecks of tobacco from his lip. "Sure. But that came afterwards. Last year he was still a Diamond T man. He went on a drive to Cheyenne for Diamond T, met Louella, married her and brought her back here. Nina Telfors never forgave Luke for that."

"N. Telfors," Lou muttered, thinking back to the posters he had read. "Nina Telfors?"

"Boss of Diamond T." Baxter's voice held an ugly edge. "Don't underestimate her. Behind that beautiful face is a woman as hard as nails—arrogant, spoiled and deadlier than any of the dozen gunmen she's got working for her."

"She sounds interesting," Lou commented. He stood up and walked to the window and turned to face the frowning man. Outside, the wind howled with a high wailing sound; sand skittered across the adobe sill as a gust swirled in through the window.

Baxter watched him. A dangerous man, he thought shrewdly, because he took things quietly, absorbing them and examining them with unhurried judgment.

A man he'd like to have on his side, he decided.

He stood up. "I'm expecting four men," he said. "I thought you were one of them."

Lou didn't say anything. Baxter shrugged, walked to the door. Then he stopped, forced a small smile to his lips.

"I pay three hundred a month. I can use you."

"What for?" Lou's voice held a thin curiosity.

"Your gun." Baxter reached up and touched the disfiguring scar; his eyes burned with a hatred that lay just below the surface. "I know how to break Diamond T. I helped build it—and I'll break it!"

There was a quiet, cold assurance in his voice, and Lou revised his earlier opinion of this man. Will Baxter could be a dangerous man.

"If you're interested, Winters, look me up in my office. I'm over Jake's Harness Shop, two doors south of the barbershop."

Lou said quietly: "I'll think about it."

Something in his face angered Baxter. He put his back against the door and said harshly: "It's come to this, Winters. There's no middle ground in Concho Valley. If you stay, you'll work for me or else for Diamond T!"

"I might join Ace Doolin," Lou said thinly.

There was a stubborn jut to his jaw. "I told you I don't take orders well."

"You'll take them!" Baxter snapped. He let the words lie between them, like a cocked gun. "From me—or from Diamond T!"

He saw Lou's eyes go slate gray; he tried to temper his arrogance. "I'd rather it was me, Winters. I've nothing against you. But you must see how things are here—"

He opened the door, looked back again. "I go a long way for my friends. But I'm mean with my enemies. You can choose sides, Winters—or you can ride clear of Concho Valley. But make your decision tonight!"

He closed the door behind him, and Lou heard no footsteps, the man was so silent. The wind roared high over the hotel, and the sound of a million tapping grains of sand filled the room. There was a dryness that reached into a man, and Lou found himself wetting his lips.

Irritation nagged him. He checked the loads in his Colt, pulled on his coat and went out.

CHAPTER III

Kathy Hastings was doing some figuring in a ledger when Lou stopped by the desk. An assortment of cigars in open boxes on the shelf behind her caught his eye. He bought a half-dozen crooked cheroots, having taken a liking to them during the war.

"The marshal likes to talk," he commented. "He and Mr. Baxter friendly?"

Fear showed briefly in Kathy's eyes. "George—Mr. Asher—meant no harm. Mr. Baxter asked him to report any strangers who came to town—"

"Men like me?"

She licked her lips. "Yes."

"The marshal is an obliging man," he said shortly. Then, changing the subject abruptly, he asked: "Did Frank Santree stop here?"

She shook her head. "A stranger stopped by four days ago. He didn't give his name. He asked where he could reach Luke Snow. I gave him directions to Rainbow, and he left."

"Rainbow?" Lou thought of Frank, restless, searching, looking for something that lay over the horizon. Frank had been a lot like Herb Dolan, only Dolan had a quality Frank had lacked, a streak of viciousness.

He shrugged. "I understand there was a funeral

in town today. Know where I can find the preacher who attended?"

Kathy said: "Reverend Eli Stone is the only minister in Concho. He lives in the last house on Spring Street, two blocks south. . . ."

She watched him leave and the fear drained out of her, leaving her slightly shaken. She thought of George and the way he had looked when he had mentioned the marshal, and worry sharpened her thin face.

George Asher was married—but Kathy had never given up hope.

Lou paused on the hotel veranda long enough to turn up his collar, then plunged into the wind. He came out to the street between the palms, hesitated only a moment, then turned left. He had his hat brim tugged low to protect his slitted eyes; he didn't see the rider waiting in the alley across the street.

Halfway down the block Lou turned and stepped off the walk. He bucked the wind, not expecting trouble. He didn't see the horseman until the man was almost on top of him.

Instinct saved him. He whirled and dived for the ground, and the gun flared murkily above him. The explosion was whipped away by the wind. The animal shied from the blast close to its ear and spoiled the rider's second shot. The bullet burned Lou's cheek, kicked sand into his eyes.

He kept rolling toward the walk, lurched to his

knees. The rider was plunging past—he caught a glimpse of Bowie's face, turned back to him. Then the man faded into the swirling dust. . . .

Lou came to his feet. He heard someone shout, but couldn't see anyone. He touched his cheek; sand grated under his fingers and irritated the cut.

He'd have to be more careful, he thought grimly.

He stepped back and whirled as a figure loomed up in the murk. His muzzle stopped the running man, who flung up a hand. "Hold it, Winters. It's me—the town marshal!"

Winters said: "Come ahead—slow!" He waited until he could make out Asher's white face, then slid the gun back into holster.

"Heard the shots," George said, breathing through his teeth. "I was in the barbershop. Ran out and—" He ducked his face to protect it from a hard gust of wind. When it passed he turned, asked sharply: "You run into trouble?"

Lou touched his cheek. "Yeah." He didn't trust this man; he didn't like a man who played flunkey.

"Tell Will Baxter I made my decision," he snarled. "Tell him to go to blazes!"

He turned on his heel and stalked across the street. George Asher stared after him, lips pulled tight against his teeth. His hand slid down over his gun butt, and then it was too late—Lou's tall striding figure had turned the corner.

• • •

Reverend Stone was a transplanted New Englander. He lived in a white-painted clapboard house surrounded by a white picket fence, and it was a short walk from his place to the church.

Lou used the black iron knocker on the door and waited, coat collar partially protecting him from the wind.

The door opened and a tall, gaunt man looked out at him. He filled the doorway, his gaze searching Winters, his brows pulling together in slight frown.

"Reverend Stone?"

The minister nodded.

"I'm Lou Winters. I was a friend of Frank Santree. I'd like to see Mrs. Snow."

Reverend Stone's eyes narrowed. "How did you know—?"

"I saw you drive into town ahead of me," Lou interrupted. "Is she here?"

Stone nodded. "She is." He made a quick gesture. "Come in, man. It's blowing too hard for comfort."

Lou followed him into the front room. It was small, and heavy furniture made it seem smaller. Lace antimacassars decorated the backs of the sofa and chairs; they gave a sense of stiffness to the room.

The woman he had seen riding with the Reverend was seated across a small table from an older, frail person Lou assumed was Mrs. Stone. She was sitting on the edge of her chair, a tea cup and saucer resting in her lap. It seemed to Lou as he looked at her that she was not interested in either the tea or the other woman's conversation; she sat in the seclusion of her thoughts, a quiet immobility glazing her face.

Reverend Stone took his hat and hung it on a coat tree. His tone was friendly.

"My wife, Amy—and Mrs. Snow. Louella—this is Lou Winters. He says he was a friend of Frank Santree."

A tremor went through the woman. She put her cup down on the table and turned to face him; a flicker of interest cracked her impassivity. With some surprise Lou saw she was a young woman; he had expected someone older.

"Lou Winters," she repeated. "Oh, yes—Frank mentioned you."

"He was my partner," Lou said. He was standing by the head of the small table, between the two women. He was conscious of the scratch on his cheek and the gun on his hip.

"He was supposed to meet me in Salinas," he added. "When he didn't show up, I came here to find out why."

"Frank was buried this afternoon," Louella said. Her voice was a flat monotone. "Beside my husband."

Lou knuckled his jaw. "I heard."

She looked up quickly, surprise brightening her gaze. Behind him Reverend Stone said: "You knew about the hanging?"

"I was told," he said flatly. "By some Diamond T riders, in Tom's Bar—"

He saw Reverend Stone stiffen and eye him with a sudden frowning regard. Louella Snow set her cup down, a bright new appraisal in her gaze.

"Then you're the man who killed Sam Keeler?" Stone said.

Lou nodded. "You know the story, then, Reverend."

The minister flung up an arm in an impatient gesture. "Tom is a friend. He sent Tony with the news—" He took a turn which brought him behind his seated wife and facing Lou.

"You're in trouble," he said bluntly. "If you take my advice, you'll leave town soon as this storm blows over, and keep riding, Mr. Winters."

"That's what Charley Mizner told me," Lou said. He didn't seem disturbed or worried. He smiled faintly. "So far you're the third man to tell me to get out of Concho."

"It's good advice," Reverend Stone said bluntly. "There's enough trouble in the valley now." He glanced at Louella and sighed softly. "Too many people have been hurt and feel they should take matters of justice into their own hands. A newcomer like you can only make things worse."

"Frank Santree was my partner," Lou said

stubbornly. "He came into Concho Valley to see an old friend of his, and Diamond T hung him. Reverend, even if they admit it was all a mistake, it won't help Frank. I didn't know Luke Snow myself. Maybe he was rustling Diamond T beef—"

"Luke never touched another man's cows!" Louella cut in. There was an angry note in her voice.

Lou looked at her, nodded. "I'm inclined to believe that, ma'am. And I know Frank was no rustler. That's why I'm staying—"

"Winters!" Reverend Stone's voice sounded tired. "What can you do for Frank Santree now? He's dead—"

"I can send him company!" Lou said bleakly. "It might not do Frank any good, but when I ride out of here I'll ride easy."

Stone threw up his hands. His wife smiled uneasily and took advantage of this moment of silence to ask Lou if he would like tea.

Lou shook his head. "Some other time, Mrs. Stone. I shouldn't have intruded on you. But I came to see Luke's widow. I wanted to ask her how Frank died."

Louella lifted her shoulders. "There's little I can tell you. Luke and Frank rode away during the morning. When they didn't get back that night, I knew something had happened."

Lou frowned. "That all?"

"Charley Mizner, with a half-dozen Diamond T riders flanking him, drove a wagon into Rainbow's yard the next morning. They dropped Luke and Frank off in front of my door—" Her voice held a flat, unforgiving note. "I'll never forget that, Winters!"

A silence followed, uneasy with things unspoken. Reverend Stone looked sad and angry and somewhat helpless. Lou had the feeling Stone had tried and had been unable to reach this woman—and studying her cold, set features, he sensed an unyielding bitterness, a deep strength of purpose, that struck a note of understanding in him.

This was no weak woman, groping and uncertain after her husband's death. If Diamond T had been after Rainbow, they still had this woman to deal with.

The silence began to drag awkwardly, and he knew now that Louella Snow had nothing more to say to him. Not here or now.

So he said softly: "Thank you for telling me, Mrs. Snow." He turned to the Reverend and his wife. "My apologies for this intrusion—"

Mrs. Stone smiled faintly. "It was no intrusion. And please stay awhile longer. This horrible windstorm—" She made a helpless gesture.

"It may well last until morning," Lou pointed out. "Thank you again." He started for the door, and Louella called after him:

"Mr. Winters! I'm curious. You say you were warned to leave Concho Valley. Do you intend to leave?"

"Not right away," Lou answered briefly. He smiled. "I'll be staying at the hotel. If Frank left anything at Rainbow you think I should have—"

"I'll see that you get it," she finished. He thought he saw a smile in her eyes.

Reverend Stone saw him to the door. "I wish you'd take my advice, Winters. No good can come of your staying."

Lou faced him. Anger stirred briefly in his eyes. "What's the matter, Reverend? Are you afraid of Diamond T?"

"I've no cause," Stone said stiffly. "But violence has a habit of spreading. Diamond T has few friends in Concho, and Nina Telfors has none. If a mistake was made in the case of Luke and your partner, then the law—"

"What law?" Lou asked harshly. "I've met your town marshal."

"I didn't mean George Asher," Stone said. "I've written to the sheriff at Gunsight to send an investigator—" He put a hand on Lou's arm.

"Think about it first, Winters. Sentiment in town is all against Diamond T. Miss Telfors is a headstrong girl, a strange girl and essentially, I believe, a lonely girl, too proud to admit her loneliness. And she can be used by unscrupulous persons."

Lou nodded, his voice curiously strained. "I've heard of Miss Telfors. You're the first to sympathize with her."

"She needs it," Reverend Stone said abruptly.

Lou glanced past him in the direction of the front room. "Luke's widow could stand some sympathy, too, I reckon."

Reverend Stone shook his head. "Louella's too strong for that. Understanding, perhaps—but not sympathy." He put out his hand. "I'd rather you left, Winters. But if you stay, come again—"

He watched the rangy man leave, fade into the murky afternoon. A dismal foreboding settled over him. The storm blowing across Concho Valley was only a mild forerunner of the violence that would follow. . . .

CHAPTER IV

Will Baxter kicked the stool out of his way as he walked to the window which looked down on Main Street. It was a small office, well furnished, with Currier and Ives prints on the walls. Heavy legal tomes stood between black basalt elephant bookends on his desk. But the glass-enclosed bookcase was gathering dust, and he had not opened a law book in months.

Once he had spent more time at the county seat than in his office; now he felt restless and bitter, a man with time on his hands.

The wind rattled on loose panes, and somewhere in the building a loose board banged. . . . He stood and gazed down on the obscured street, not looking for anyone, although he had been expecting four men this week.

He had lost weight. His clothes hung loosely on his slight frame, and the hollows in his cheeks looked more pronounced because of the flaring of his nostrils.

He had taken down the "Attorney at Law" after his name and substituted "Specialist in Land Titles." He had not realized what his law diploma meant to him until he lost it.

The wind blew in wild swirls across the street. He knew from experience that it would blow like this until sundown, ease off for an hour or so and pick up again during the night. It might still be blowing in the morning.

Baxter knew this country as well as most of Concho's five hundred inhabitants. He had come here fifteen years before, a young, eager lawyer from the East. He was not old now, but he gave the impression of age. There was no quickness in his eyes, and self-pity had put lines around his mouth. In time the self-pity had changed to deep, corroding hate.

Baxter had come to Concho Valley before the Telforses, at a time when old John Pedrick had owned what was now Diamond T. He had been a young man then, fresh out of law school and with ambition more ingrained than ideals; a sharp, clever lawyer with one major weakness. He had a tendency to answer "Yes, sir!" quickly and to bow to money, because money was what he was after.

Money, not power! It had been his great mistake, he thought now, and bitterness ran like a fault through the lines of his face. He had wanted money, not power—and in the end he had gained neither.

He heard the door open, but he knew who it was and he didn't turn. Boots scraped hesitantly on the worn floor boards. Then Asher's voice came, with its usual note of hesitation when he addressed Baxter.

"He's headed for Reverend Stone's house. . . ."

Will turned around. George stood facing him. The marshal had his hat pushed back on his curly brown hair, and as always, Baxter reacted to the stubborn boyishness of that face. He couldn't really count on this man who had married his sister. George was not a man for violence, though he could use his fists or his gun when the issue was unavoidable. He was not physically a coward; but violence, Baxter had found out, was a trait apart from courage.

He made a quick gesture. "Let him. He won't find out anything he doesn't already know."

"He probably knows more than we think," George said. He fished in his shirt pocket for the makings and rolled a cigaret with the brooding distraction of a man whose mind was on other things. "Someone tried to shoot him a few minutes ago. It looked like Sid Bowie to me, but I can't swear to it—"

"Diamond T!" Baxter's eyes flashed. "Diamond T riders were in town?"

"They were up on the butte when the funeral was going on," Asher said grimly. "I saw them myself. But I didn't think they'd come to town."

"Bowie!" Baxter repeated. His brows knitted. "If Bowie was in town, then Sam Keeler was with him. Bowie never went anywhere without Sam."

Asher grinned faintly. "This is one time when Bowie ain't anxious to join Sam." He stuck his cigaret into a corner of his mouth and cupped a match to it.

"Will," he said bitterly, "don't push this hombre Winters!"

"What in the devil are you talking about?" Baxter demanded roughly. He walked up to the marshal, faced him. "What's this about Sam?"

"He's dead!" Asher's flat assurance crumbled. "I just came from Tom Sands' place. I found out Winters checked in there, asking for Frank Santree. Bowie and Sam Keeler walked in a coupla minutes later, and the way Tom tells it, they forced Winters into a shootout. Charley Mizner came in just before the fight, looking for Sam and Bowie, and was treated pretty rough by Winters. Tom says he helped Charley pack Sam's body into Charley's buggy, but Bowie didn't leave town with them. Looks like he figgered to even things for Sam."

Baxter absorbed this long speech slowly. The marshal moved his shoulders, as though trying to shift a heavy load on them. "He said he's looking for Ace Doolin, Will. Why? You know, and I know, he won't find Doolin here. Far as I know Doolin's in purgatory—"

"Keep what you know to yourself!" Baxter snapped. "I don't give a hang why Winters is in town. Maybe he came for Frank Santree. I'm only interested in one thing. What is he going to do now!"

"He won't run," Asher said. His voice held a stubborn insistence. "Don't push him, Will."

Baxter threw up his hands. "George, George! When are you going to grow up? A man like that doesn't sit on the fence. I offered him a job. If he stays he'll have to take it! Or he'll work for Diamond T. There'll be no middle ground!"

George Asher licked his lips; his cigaret jerked loosely in the corner of his mouth and trailed ashes.

"You know how I feel, Will. I don't want to be caught in the middle, either. Are you sure that's what you want? Will breaking Diamond T be enough?"

Involuntarily Baxter's fingers reached up to the white scar slashing across his cheek. "I don't know, George." In that moment he was honest, searching within himself for answers. "I'll answer that when I've broken Diamond T; when I see Nina Telfors walk down this street and take the stage out of Concho Valley for good!"

George sucked in a shallow breath. "My sympathies are with you, Will. You know that. And it's not only because of Mary. Practically every man in town who doesn't owe his soul to Diamond T is on your side. But I remember once when you used to speak of ideals—"

"Ideals are for fools!" Will cut in harshly. "Only the powerful can really afford them. They can make fine talk about law and order and justice, but guns are what makes those words stick, George. I know. Diamond T got big because of the guns Lord Telfors hired—and my brains. Now I'm going to take it away from his daughter!"

The marshal let out a slow breath. "You know the law, Will. But you might find yourself taking on more than you can handle—"

"I'll handle it!" Baxter cut him off contemptuously. "Laws are made for small people, George—men like you! Big men use the laws to suit themselves!"

Asher's pale gaze showed a flicker of resentment, but he pushed it back. "I don't know much about the law," he admitted. "The people of Concho wanted a man who would keep the drunks off the streets and stop them from making trouble, who'd check minor offenders. I know my job. It doesn't pay much, and it doesn't have much of a future. But I sleep nights."

"Does Mary?" Baxter's tone was mocking.

George stiffened. "She should. But she's your sister. And she hates Nina Telfors." He backed to the door, shook his head bitterly. "No, she doesn't sleep well, Will. Does that satisfy you?"

"Mary's all right!" Baxter snapped. "Treat her well. And when I take over Diamond T, I'll see you get a better break than being a hundred-and-fifty-a-month town marshal."

George started to say something, decided against it. He nodded and went out, and Will heard his steps on the creaky boards; then silence took over the empty office, and even the windstorm seemed far away.

He walked to the cupboard and took out a bottle of Bourbon and a glass and set them down on the desk. He sank down in the swivel chair and poured slowly. Baxter was not a drinking man. Up until a few months ago he had never taken anything harder than beer—but that had been another life.

He put the drink away in a fast gulp and settled back, his eyes filming with bitter thoughts. He ran back over the years, sorting out his mistakes, baring the hidden corners of his soul.

George was wrong. He had never been a man of ideals, of principle, but rather a man who had paid lip service to them. He had used the right phrases because he'd thought they sounded well. But he'd had a streak of subservience in him that Lord Telfors had sensed and used.

Telfors had held out the bait of money, which was Will Baxter's real goal, and when Telfors had no further use for him the arrogant boss of Diamond T had dumped him.

Telfors had done a thorough, cold-blooded job. He had framed Baxter on a bribery charge, and had used his influence at the state capital to get Baxter disbarred.

It was one of Telfors' last acts; he had died of a heart attack two weeks later.

It had taken Will Baxter a while to get over the shock. He had come to consider himself an essential part of Diamond T, even above Charley Mizner, and his dismissal and subsequent disgrace nearly finished him. Only Telfors' death, shortly afterward, finally roused him.

With Telfors dead, he thought he had a chance to make a deal with Charley Mizner. He had not even considered Nina Telfors, whom he considered a spoiled, irresponsible child.

Now he touched the old scar on his face, remembering, through the clear recollection of pain, the sharp cut of her riding quirt; hearing again the acid contempt in her voice.

"Get him out of here, Charley! See that he never bothers me again!"

He remembered it clearly, seeing himself on his knees in the yard by the wide portico of the ugly stone house Lord Telfors had built . . . watching himself writhe in pain as Nina Telfors turned arrogantly away from him and went inside.

They had put him on his horse and Charley had ridden with him to the far gate. Nina Telfors thought she had gotten rid of him then, but the pattern of disaster had really started there, in the dust of the Diamond T yard.

Winters bucked the punishing wind to Main Street, paused briefly to consider his position, and caught a glimpse of a sign across the street which reminded him he had not eaten since morning. There was a long-legged bay horse at the rack, tailing the wind. . . . Lou had passed this way not more than twenty minutes before and he had not seen a horse in front of POP HOLLAND'S CAFÉ.

He crossed the street, brushing close to the skittish animal, and ran his hand across the flank. Stepping up to the walk, he knew that the bronc had been ridden hard and only recently tied to the bar.

The brand was a small Crescent; he thought he recalled the brand as a north country one, but he wasn't sure. It wasn't Diamond T, and he relaxed slightly as he pushed open the door of the café.

The wind scattered sand through the restaurant, lifted the corners of the tablecloths on the half-dozen tables, and died abruptly as he closed the door. He stood with his back to it for a brief moment, surveying the almost empty room.

There was a long, dusty slat of a man on the end stool, facing so that he could watch the door. A fat, sweating, sloppy man, with a fringe of gray hair around a shining bald top, was just placing a bowl of chili in front of him.

The stranger was the only customer. He measured Lou through quick, yellow-green eyes that slitted with the lazy regard of a big cat; something about Lou disturbed him. His hand slipped casually from the counter top and rested lightly on his knee, a few inches from the handle of a Frontier Colt snugged in a thonged-down holster.

He nodded a friendly greeting as Lou approached. "Howdy." He had a Texas drawl. "Pop's been complaining about business. Join me in a cup of coffee?"

Lou smiled. "I'm a stranger in town myself. Glad to have company." He looked at Pop, who was leaning over the counter. "I'll have a steak to go with the coffee—and all the trimmings you got advertised on that Special tacked to the wall."

"Take a while on that steak," Pop growled discourteously. "Chili's quicker. And only two bits."

Lou took a five-dollar bill out of his pocket and put it on the counter. "I want a steak, not chili. And I'm not going anywhere, so take your time—"

Pop shrugged. "I'll see what Sanchez can do. Coffee now?"

Lou nodded. He turned and caught the other man's eyes on him. They crinkled in a smile, but there was a watchful glint in their yellow depths.

"Cussed storm," the man said. "Got caught coming through Morgan's Pass and ducked into a hole, waiting for it to blow over. Waited a couple of hours, but it grew worse." He chuckled. "Figgered I'd better make a ride for it, or get buried alive. . . ." He took a spoonful of the chili, made a face, and reached for the hot pepper.

Lou waited. The man was leading up to something, and he had an idea what.

But the gunman seemed content with that. Pop came over with Lou's coffee, pushed the sugar bowl toward him, and went back into the kitchen. Someone protested angrily in Mexican.

Pop came out again and leaned against the counter, staring moodily at the storm outside.

"Say, does it always blow like that, Pop?" The gunman seemed garrulous, eager to be friendly. But his eyes didn't laugh, and Lou noticed that he continued to watch the door.

"Two or three times a year," Pop said indifferently. He ran a sweaty palm across the top of his head. "Dumps half the desert east of here into the valley each time it blows."

The gunman turned to Lou. "Heard it was good cattle country down here. Feller who told me must have been a liar."

"It is!" Pop defended his home, rousing himself. "We've got one of the biggest ranches in the Territory located in the valley."

The gunman pushed his bowl of chili away and started to roll himself a cigaret. "Ain't seen much of it," he admitted. He put his glance on the café owner. "I'm looking for a job. Can break a bronc with the best of them. What did you say the name of this spread was?"

"Diamond T—" Pop let his glance run down the gunman's body to the Colt under his right forearm; his gaze jerked over to Lou's gun set down low and with the same cold authority. "They might hire you," he said, "both of you."

"Count me out," Lou said, grinning. "I've had enough of punching another man's cows."

"I can't afford the sentiment," the gunman said. He looked Lou over with sharp expectancy as he rose, dropped a silver dollar on the counter. "Nice to have run into you, fella."

Lou's smile lingered. "Knowles send you?" he asked innocently.

The gunman stiffened slightly and the look of easy friendliness left him. He said softly: "You know Zig Knowles?"

"Never met the man." Lou chuckled. "But you'll find Will Baxter's office up the street, over Jake's Harness Shop. He's expecting you."

The tall gunster eyed him, trying to read behind Lou's grin. The fake good nature was gone; his eyes held a narrow, bleak distrust. He ran the edge of his thumbnail slowly across the tawny bristle on his jaw.

"Thanks for the directions," he said. His voice was cool. "I'll see you around."

Lou nodded. "Maybe." He watched the man walk out. The wind seemed to have died down somewhat in the interval. He glimpsed the gunman through the window, stepping up into saddle of the bay horse, whirling him away with a savage hand.

Then he turned and caught Pop Holland staring. The fat man roused and went into the kitchen and came out a few moments later with Lou's steak. He placed the meal down in front of Lou and edged away, busying himself with dirty glasses. Fear seemed to have laid a bar of caution over his tongue.

CHAPTER V

Sundown's long shadows marched in on the heels of the dying windstorm. The sandstone hills appeared in the clearing air, sharp against the western end of town. Sentinel Butte loomed massively to the northwest, its flat top fading back and breaking into a hundred twisting canyons toward the Broken Butte country.

There was a dry, irritating stillness in the air. Lou felt the brittle dryness crack his skin as he paused on the walk outside the cafe. Sounds seemed uncommonly loud. The clang of a blacksmith's hammer rang through town; the rasping of a sticking window came clearly.

There were people on the walks now, and here and there shopkeepers were out, sweeping sand across the walks into the street.

Lou put his attention on the bay tied to the harness shop rack. The gunman had gone straight to Baxter, and if he was the first to arrive, the others would be in shortly. He wondered why Baxter hated Diamond T. Big ranches inevitably made enemies, but he had gathered from Baxter's guarded talk that it was Nina Telfors whom Baxter hated.

He took a cigar from his pocket and lighted up. A rider topped the rise beyond the bank and came jogging down Main Street. He rode loosely in the saddle, his body jouncing easily to the animal's gait. He rode with his eyes taking in both sides of the street and with the polished stock of a Winchester jutting high from a saddle scabbard.

Lou watched him ride by. The stranger gave Lou a long, hard look. He was a wiry, buck-toothed youngster, freckles plain across his face; a seedy-looking boy of twenty in sun-faded, dust-caked range clothes. A brass-studded wide belt cinched in a narrow waist, but Lou noticed that the pair of pearl-handled Colts he wore were worth more than the sorry-looking dun mare he rode, or the rest of his personal belongings.

The newcomer kept his gaze on Lou for a long moment, then shifted it to the bay horse tied to the harness shop bar. He seemed to recognize the animal, for he frowned slightly and touched spurs to the mare, lifting her to a faster gait.

Lou watched him step down by the bay horse, tie it up with casual air, glance up to the window where "WILL BAXTER, Specialist in Land Titles," was painted across the panes. Then he headed up the long flight of outside stairs to Baxter's office.

That's two, Lou mused. Knowles knows his gunslingers. If that isn't Reb Myers I'll eat my—

From the corner of his eye he saw George Asher step out of the barbershop, throw him a quick look, then put his attention on the man climbing the stairs to Baxter's office. He stood there, a stocky man, the badge prominent on his vest.

Lou waited, and after a while George ducked back into the barbershop. Winters smiled. He turned and headed up the street, and within a few minutes found himself on the outskirts of town. The road faded across the bare flats, angling toward Sentinel Butte and the cut of Morgan's Pass. . . . The wooden headboards on top of the small hill caught his attention, and on impulse he headed up the rutted road leading to the cemetery.

Five minutes later he paused by the two new graves. Neither was graced as yet by a marker; there was nothing to indicate to Lou which grave held Frank's body.

He stood before them and thought of Louella Snow. She had not told him everything. She had not told him why her husband and Frank had ridden to Diamond T. . . . She was holding something back.

Then he heard someone coming up the hill and turned, his hand instinctively brushing over the walnut butt of his Colt.

George Asher stopped. He looked small and chunky standing in the ruts of the road; there was doggedness in his stance.

"Saw you headed this way," he explained shortly. "I want to talk with you."

"I'm listening." Lou's voice was equally short.

"Will told me he had a talk with you. He thought you were one of the men he'd sent for—"

"And you?"

"I thought so, too." Asher's voice held a faint hostility. "Baxter's my brother-in-law, Winters. He got a raw deal from Diamond T. He wants to get even."

Lou waited. The marshal was trying to get at something, but he was having trouble. He stood in the middle of the road while behind him figures moved in town, small and diminished by distance.

"I don't give a hang about Diamond T," Asher said finally. "The girl bossing that bunch of tough gunhands ain't got the responsibility of an alley cat. But I don't want to see Baxter get hurt. He thinks he can buck Nina Telfors, hurt her . . . he's hiring guns to do it."

Lou frowned. "Why tell me, Marshal?"

"Because I don't know where you stand!" There was sharpness now in the marshal's tone.

Lou looked down at the near grave; he scuffed sand from the small mound with his toe. "A friend of mine is in one of these graves, Marshal. Frank Santree."

"I heard." Asher's voice was cold. "I heard you had a run-in with Charley Mizner and a couple of Diamond T gunhands in Tom's Bar. Heard you killed one of them—Sam Keeler!"

Lou shrugged. "If you heard that much you heard they pushed it, Marshal."

"I didn't come up here because of that," Asher said. "Keeler's had that slug coming for a long time. But where Keeler went, Bowie went. Now Sid Bowie's alone. Might do you good to remember that, Winters!"

Lou studied the man, unable to make him out. There was hostility in him, and yet he was warning Lou. Lou nodded slowly. "Thanks, Marshal. I'll remember."

Asher made a small, resigned gesture. His face looked suddenly old, as if an inner fatigue had broken through. "I came up here to ask you to leave town. I've got nothing against you, Winters. But I've got a job to do. It ain't a big job—" He turned and gestured to the town below. "Just from one end of that street to the other—from the bank to the church. I'm a small man, Winters. I know it—and I've been told. Diamond T runs the valley. But down there, long as I wear this badge, I'm boss. I want you to know that, Winters. *I'm boss!* Not Will Baxter, nor any of the guns he has hired! Not even Nina Telfors!"

He turned and walked away, his shoulders sagging slightly . . . but there was a steadiness to his walk, and a sort of rock-like purpose to his body, that gave Lou Winters a new insight into the man.

• • •

Night came in layers, pushing the brightness from the sky, leaving only a thin rim of light on the western horizon. Then this too vanished, and the stars leaped out through the vault of night, and a moon tilted on one crescent rose over the dark hills.

Lou Winters lingered over his glass of beer in Tom's Bar. He had gone back there after leaving the cemetery. The saloon held a fair crowd, but the customers seemed clannishly grouped. Lou leaned against the bar and considered his course of action.

It was Doolin he still wanted, and to the best of his knowledge Doolin was hiding out in Mexico. But Doolin might have slipped back across the border. Frank might have heard something from Luke—

He interrupted his thoughts to study the old man at the table by the wall. It was the same man who had been in the saloon when he had had his ruckus with Diamond T. He had almost finished whittling his boat, and Lou revised his earlier estimate of the man. He was not as old as his grizzled features would indicate, or as senile. Once he caught a quick levelling of the man's eyes on him and sensed a sharp scrutiny before a vacant look came back into them.

Lou had another beer and smoked his cigar and then sat in on a game of poker with a farmer and a rancher on the Quicksilver and two townsmen. One was the local dentist, a fat, boisterous man with bad teeth who worked in the blacksmith shop when his business was poor; the other a barber.

There was little mention of Diamond T, or the hanging of Luke and Frank. The funeral that had taken place that day might never have happened as far as these men were concerned.

Lou idly mentioned the reward poster he had seen on his way to town, and the bib-overalled farmer, who called himself Gillian, lifted a frowning face from his cards.

"Ace Doolin ain't never bothered me, fella."

"You ever see him?"

"Doolin?" The farmer grinned. "I don't think there is such a man. But you ask Farley here. He claims he saw Doolin."

Farley was the rancher, a thin, nervous man with a habit of pinching the bridge of his nose in a tired gesture.

"I didn't see him," Farley denied. "But my hired hand did. Slim saw Doolin and a couple of his owlhooters ride across Luke's place a week ago. That's Rainbow, fella. Slim says it looked like they had been seeing Luke—"

"That's the hombre Diamond T hanged, I hear," Lou said. His voice was casual.

"Maybe they knew what they were doing," Farley said. His voice rose angrily. "Yeah, I know how you all feel about Diamond T. But they ain't bothered me. And they haven't bothered any of you, either—"

"Ride across Diamond T range," the swarthy barber sneered, "and see what happens. Old 'High and Mighty' Telfors was bad enough, with his airs and accent you hardly could understand. But his daughter—"

Farley subsided, putting his attention on his cards. "I never really trusted Luke," he mumbled. "He rode for Diamond T for years; then all at once he sets up with a spread of his own. And about the same time this Ace Doolin moves in the Broken Buttes and starts raiding Diamond T—"

"This Ace Doolin," Lou interrupted, "what's he look like?"

"Like it says on the poster by the marshal's office, fella." Farley looked at Lou with growing curiosity. "Rangy fella, light blue eyes, sandy hair, weighs about a hundred and seventy, stands about six feet. Has a gold-capped tooth up front—"

Surprise touched Winters. This was Doolin, a fairly accurate description of the man he had known as Herb Dolan.

"I read the poster, too," Gillian said. "But I ain't ever seen the man."

"Slim did. He described him." Farley threw down his cards. "But I didn't come to town to talk about Doolin."

"Sorry," Lou cut in quietly.

Farley looked at him with truculent hostility. "You know this outlaw?"

"Only by reputation," Lou answered. "I rode through a town up north of here where he and five men raided the bank. They killed the teller, a woman and two other men and got away with sixty thousand dollars. There's a reward of five thousand dollars out for him."

"I didn't know that," Gillian said sharply. "Never really knew who this Doolin jasper was. Thought he was something Diamond T made up—"

"He's out there all right," Farley interjected coldly. "Slim saw him. And if I had any money in this bank, I'd be worried about that instead of cussing Diamond T!"

Gillian flushed. "Appears that Telfors girl's been playing up to you lately."

"That's a lie!" Farley snapped. He seemed agitated, and his eyes kept blinking. "Just because I don't treat her like—like—"

"Just remember what Will Baxter got," the barber cut in sneeringly. "He was friendly with her, too."

Farley flung his cards across the table and got up. "To blazes with all of you!" he snarled. He turned and went out, walking stiffly, a man in a blind rage.

The dentist chuckled. "You jabbed his sore spot

again, Ned," he said to Gillian. "When you going to let up on him?"

Gillian shrugged. "When the pore fool quits mooning over that she-devil who's running Diamond T!"

His voice was low, but Winters straightened slowly, catching the ugly note in the man's voice, sensing something extremely personal in his words.

The barber snorted, and the dentist wiped his lips. "Man who tames that wildcat might have a handful," he said grudgingly. He added quickly, "I wouldn't even try—I ain't got that kind of stamina."

"Or the hopes," the barber said. He was a swarthy man with a sour outlook. He tossed his cards down and got up. "Count me out, too."

The game broke up with that. Lou counted his money, saw that he had won two dollars. He walked to the bar, put the money on the counter.

"See that the old feller by the wall—" he indicated the grizzled whittler—"gets a few drinks out of this."

The bartender nodded. "Friend of yours?"

"Never saw him before," Lou said. "Thought he was an old-timer here."

"Came in yesterday," the bartender said, frowning; "just before the storm. Nobody knows him. Spends his time in here. Buys a beer and whittles."

“Harmless, anyway,” Lou said. He turned and caught the grizzled man’s gaze on him. He waved briefly, smiled.

The man looked at him with unblinking gaze, then went back to his whittling. . . .

Lou walked back toward the hotel. The wind was rising again, but without its daytime fury.

He saw two riders come down the street, jogging slowly, scanning the building line as Reb Myers had done. They looked like brothers—lean, wire-hard men, with a penchant for dark clothes. The guns glinting on their hips marked them.

They rode with wary alertness. Lou eased into the deep shadows of a darkened doorway and waited until they rode by.

Baxter’s men had arrived!

He reached the adobe archway of the hotel and paused briefly under the palms. The fronds rustled dryly above him.

He considered what he had heard in Tom’s Bar. He was aware now of an undercurrent of hate in Concho Valley, of jealousy and desire, focusing on a girl he had never seen.

Nina Telfors. The picture he had of her was not good.

He thought of Frank and Luke, and now he wasn’t sure. Slim had described Ace Doolin and hinted that he had visited Luke Snow. . . .

He thought of the package he had left in the hotel safe, and the reasons he had for finding Doolin. Frank had known, but Frank was dead. Had he told Luke Snow? Was that part of the reason both men had died?

He found no answers under the rustling palm fronds. The night wind was chilly; he shrugged and turned through the gate, toward the hotel entrance.

CHAPTER VI

The lobby was dark. Light from the lamp on the desk cast only a dim glow that reached to the door; the flame flickered at his entrance, and shadows danced along the high walls.

Lou headed for the desk and his key. Kathy was nowhere in sight, although he could hear someone moving about in the back room just off the counter and pigeonhole area.

He reached the desk and was about to palm the bell when he saw his key on the book within easy reach. He leaned across the counter and flipped it free, and then he heard movement behind him.

He swung around fast, and the lamplight glinted with ominous coldness from the muzzle he leveled at the shadow.

Louella Snow came toward him, ignoring the leveled gun. Her voice was faintly amused.

"You're a quick man, Mr. Winters, and a suspicious one."

"I find it helps," Lou said. He looked at her as she came into the bright aura of the lamp. Standing, she was only a few inches shorter than he. She gave the impression of competence, of knowing what she wanted. She seemed to have broken through the stony shock of grief; her eyes had dancing lights that gave mobility to her face. She was not a beautiful girl, but there was a blunt, likable quality to her features.

"I've asked a few questions since you left the Reverend's house," she said. "You interest me."

"In a nice way, I hope," he said courteously.

"It depends," she answered. "You look too cynical to be an easy man to deal with. You're not like Luke at all."

His smile held, but his voice had an edge of distrust. "Surely you didn't come here to compare me with your late husband."

"No. There are not many men like Luke." She glanced across the counter to the rear door, which had opened a few inches.

"I'd like to talk with you," she suggested.

"Here?"

She turned and indicated the stairs. "You have a room?"

He nodded, his eyes holding a skeptical amusement. "If you don't mind—"

"I'm past minding," she cut in shortly.

Kathy Hastings came out of the back room as they went up the staircase. She watched them go, her eyes dark, secret malice twisting her lips.

Louella Snow walked to the window as Winters scraped a match and tilted the glass chimney of the lamp. The flame strengthened and cast its shadows in the square room; he looked up and saw her with her back to him. Her shoulders were stiff. He turned and closed the door, and when he swung around she was facing him.

"Frank knew Ace Doolin, didn't he?"

The question caught him by surprise. He nodded slowly. "Frank did. So did I."

She had not expected this; it showed in her face. She made a cold gesture of disbelief. "I hadn't considered it before," she said. "But if Frank was a friend of that outlaw—"

"He wasn't," Lou headed her off. He walked over to her. "Is that what you wanted to know?"

"Part of it," she admitted. She met his glance and measured him; there was a directness about this woman that Lou admired.

"I don't believe Ace Doolin is in Concho Valley," she said defiantly.

"Neither do I," Lou answered. He smiled wryly. "At least I didn't until a few minutes ago."

"Charley Mizner said Luke was in with Doolin," she said bitterly. "They caught him and Frank in a raid and hung them. That's the excuse they gave. But if there isn't any Ace Doolin—"

"There is," Lou cut in grimly. "But I'm not sure he's in Concho Valley."

She turned away from him and sat down on the bed. "I don't care about Doolin," she said softly. "Some things Luke didn't tell me. I know he had been worried about something for weeks. When Luke was worried he kept silent. When Frank showed up they had some sort of private conversation. Whatever was worrying Luke he told Frank. I was in the bedroom, but I heard them mention Doolin and Charley Mizner. They rode away that morning. I never saw them alive after—"

"You think the Diamond T foreman is playing his own little game with the Telfors spread?"

"Maybe. But I know why Luke was killed—and it wasn't because he was stealing Diamond T beef. Luke knew he'd have trouble when he married me and came back to Concho Valley."

"From Charley Mizner?"

"No. From Nina Telfors."

Lou took a cigar from his pocket. She was looking up at him, and he saw a change come over her face.

"Some women have everything," she said. "They never have to work. They have no worries. They're born beautiful, and men cater to them from the time they're old enough to appreciate it—"

She shrugged, a small smile curving her lips. "You think I'm jealous, Lou. In a way, I am. Nina Telfors grew up having everything. What she wanted she got. No, she wasn't in love with Luke. But he worked for her. And those who work for Nina Telfors belong to her—like her cattle, her horses. She buys them and they obey her. They don't quit Diamond T—they die or they're fired."

"But Luke quit," Lou said gently. "Is that it?"

She nodded. “Luke met me in Cheyenne. We got married. He didn’t consult Nina Telfors about it. When we came back he quit Diamond T. She never forgave him.”

Lou frowned. “What do you plan to do? Stay on at Rainbow?”

“It’s my home,” she said grimly.

“Running a ranch, even a small one, is hard work. And if you’re right about the Telfors girl, then you’ll be in trouble if you hang on.”

“Two things I had learned pretty well before I came to Concho Valley,” she said coldly. “One was how to handle a Winchester rifle. The other was how to take care of myself.”

He believed her. There was strength in this woman, an almost masculine capability. And yet behind the hardness there was a woman. . . . He wondered briefly what sort of man Luke had been.

“You might hold out,” he agreed. “But you wouldn’t get anywhere. You wouldn’t pay for Luke—”

“That’s why I’m here,” she said. “Frank Santree was your partner. Diamond T murdered him, as they killed my husband. What are you planning to do about it?”

“Find Doolin,” he murmured.

“There might not even be a Doolin,” she insisted harshly.

“Then someone is working a crooked game in

Concho Valley," he replied. "I want to find out what it is. And when I do I'll find out why Frank and Luke were framed."

"Where will you start?"

"I don't know," he answered honestly. "Will Baxter offered me a job." He smiled faintly. "He hates Nina Telfors, too."

"He has his reasons," she said. "But I'm not interested in Baxter." She got to her feet. "I can't offer you what Baxter can pay. But I need a hand on Rainbow. Will you work for me?"

He considered this. Charley Mizner had warned him to get out of Concho Valley. And Will Baxter had put it to him bluntly: Ride for Baxter or Diamond T, or leave the valley.

They had not considered that he might stay on with Rainbow.

He nodded. "You've hired a hand, Mrs. Snow."

She smiled and held out her hand. "Nina Telfors doesn't want Rainbow. She doesn't need it. But she won't like my staying on. We'll have trouble—"

"I'm looking forward to it," he said. His voice was casual, but the slant of his jaw had a stubborn tilt.

She walked to the door. "I told you everything I know about your partner, and why I believe he was hung along with Luke. Nina Telfors wanted Luke killed because he knew something about her that would destroy her if he talked. Luke told me. And when the time comes, Winters, I'll use it!"

Her tone was flat, touched with bitter triumph.

"I'm staying with the Stones tonight. Meet me there in the morning. About nine?"

He nodded. "I'll be there."

He watched her go out, a slim, stiff figure in black. . . . Her presence lingered in that cheerless room for minutes afterward.

CHAPTER VII

Lee Gates, the gunman Winters had met in POP HOLLAND'S CAFÉ, stood against the dusty bookcase, an impassive look in his eyes. Will Baxter was talking to Reb Myers, the tough kid who had just come into the office.

"Three hundred a month," he repeated harshly. "Zig Knowles must have told you what I was willing to pay!"

Myers shrugged. He wasn't visibly impressed by the offer. "Sure, Knowles told me." He glanced at Gates, studying him—they had obviously not met before. He was a distrustful man, this Myers—toughness was written all over his face. He was twenty, but he had lived with more violence than men twice his age.

"Knowles also said there was no law in Concho Valley," he muttered. He caught Gates' slow sneer out of the corners of his eyes and reacted immediately; he put his hard gunmetal gray eyes challengingly on the thin gunman, temper rising in him.

"George?" Baxter made a quick gesture of dismissal. "George's my brother-in-law. He won't bother you."

Gates said thinly: "Maybe Myers wants to know just what he's getting into, Mr. Baxter."

Will flushed. "I was going to wait until the other two got here." He saw Myers' face go hard; there was an impatient streak in the kid. "No reason why I shouldn't tell you, though," he added reasonably.

"Here's what you'll be up against. There's a big cattle outfit in the valley. Might be you've heard of Diamond T—" He looked expectantly at both men and saw no reaction. He shrugged. "Some hard men are riding for Diamond T. I don't want to give you the wrong impression about what you might be getting into. You might have to use your guns."

"Go on," Myers said insolently. "We know why we're here."

Baxter reddened, but controlled his temper. He'd have to go slow with Myers—he sensed this. He couldn't push this man or order him with a harsh tongue.

"Diamond T is run by a woman, and an Easterner named Charley Mizner." He saw a sneer break across Myers' face and he added coldly: "Don't underestimate Charley, Myers. He's more dangerous than all the men he's got riding for him."

Myers said impatiently: "I don't want histories, Mr. Baxter. I expect trouble. You wouldn't be hiring me if you didn't." He fished out of his breast pocket a thin black cigar and stuck it in the corner of his mouth. He made no move to light it.

"Just what do you want me to do? Kill somebody? This Charley Mizner? Or the woman?"

"I don't want anybody killed!" Baxter snapped. "Not yet. If you get pushed—and you will be—well, you're supposed to know how to handle that gun!"

Myers wheeled on him. He was a youngster who couldn't take opposition, and it was obvious that his gun skill was a sore spot with him.

"Supposed to nothing! This gun is my business! Don't ever question it!" He looked at Gates, found the older man eyeing him with keen interest.

"Reckon Knowles send you, too?"

Lee nodded. "Name's Lee Gates. Mr. Baxter forgot to introduce us, Myers."

Baxter snorted. He was the boss, but he found himself disconcerted by these men. A touch of uneasiness brought a cold sweat to his upper lip. Could he handle them? Once he'd broken Diamond T—and he had little doubt he could do so—he might have trouble with Reb Myers.

Lee was asking with level interest: "Just what do we have to do to earn this money, Mr. Baxter?"

"Homestead!" The word came out in a snap, pushed by Baxter's anger. He turned to the small cupboard and brought out the half-filled bottle of Bourbon and found three glasses. He poured three shots and brought one over to Gates, who was frowning.

"You and Myers," he explained, "will homestead on Dry Creek—about twelve miles from town." His grin was crooked. "It's on Diamond T range."

He turned and handed Myers his glass.

"It isn't as bad as it sounds," he assured them. "Dry Creek was old Peg Turner's place, before Diamond T bought him out. They're using it as a line shack; I think they keep a man in it part of the year. They might have a man up there now."

Myers cut in, puzzled, "You want us to jump that line shack?"

"Diamond T has no legal right to it," Baxter said. There was a triumphant glint in his eyes. "Old Turner never met the requirements for filing his homestead rights. Telfors bought the place from Turner, but it never legally belonged to Peg Turner."

Myers shook his head. "How do you know about it?"

"I was Lord Telfors' attorney for five years," Baxter answered. A trace of arrogance crept into his voice; he was on his own ground here. "I knew about Turner's lapse, but at the time it didn't matter. Same thing happened at Copper Springs. A prospector by the name of Henry Soho built a shack there. He never filed. He just moved away, and Diamond T moved in."

Gates drank his whiskey and looked into his empty glass, as if looking for an explanation of the future in it.

"How many men ride for Diamond T?" His voice was only casually interested.

"Eleven, not counting the cook and old Jess, the Negro handyman." He went back to the cupboard and picked up his glass. "I know all of them. They'll fight, but not against anyone who can give them real trouble—"

Myers cut in bluntly, "You want Gates and me to take over that line shack and file on it?"

"I already filed on it," Baxter said.

"What about that other place, Copper Springs?"

"That's a job for the other two Knowles is sending me. Same sort of deal."

Gates said: "Seems to me this job is worth more than three hundred, Mr. Baxter. Appears to me we do the killing—and maybe the dying. And you get," he smiled thinly, "the biggest spread in the valley."

Baxter studied the man. "I don't care that much about Diamond T," he said slowly. "If we win, you'll get your share of it." He touched the old scar with the tips of his fingers. "I want to break Diamond T! That's as far as I'm thinking. We'll settle shares later."

Surprisingly, Myers agreed. "Sounds all right to me." He looked at Gates. "Reckon you and me are gonna be partners. Okay with you?"

Lee nodded. He walked over and put his empty glass on the desk. "I met a hombre in Pop's café," he mentioned. "Said he was a stranger in town. Rangy feller, with a little scar under his ear. He seemed to know just why I was in town—even told me where to find you—"

"Winters!" Baxter's face congested.

"Didn't get his name," Gates said. "How does he stand in this? He with us?"

"Maybe." Baxter let out a harsh breath. "With us or against us. We'll find out in the morning."

Myers was standing by the wall, listening. The name seemed to have made some impression on him; his lips were sucked in tight against his teeth.

"He struck me as the kind of hombre I'd rather have with us," Gates muttered. "If Knowles didn't send him, what's he doing in town?"

"Claims he was a friend of a man Diamond T caught and hung two days ago." Baxter grinned wryly. "He says he's looking for Ace Doolin."

Myers snorted softly. Baxter put his attention on him. "You know Ace Doolin?"

"By reputation," the young killer answered shortly. "I didn't know he was in Concho Valley."

"I'm not so sure he is," Baxter said. He didn't elaborate. "Let's go down to Tom's Bar," he invited. "You can meet my brother-in-law, George. Don't let him bother you. He takes his badge seriously—but he does what I tell him to."

Myers' grin was wolfish. "Keep him quiet then, Mr. Baxter. I wouldn't want to have to kill him!"

There was a thin and unsettling silence in the room then—an uneasy stillness that was broken by the sound of footsteps coming up the rickety steps. Myers wheeled around and instinctively put his back to the wall; Gates stepped toward the rear of the room and faced the door.

Someone knocked. Baxter walked to the door. He opened it about half a foot, looked askance at the two shadowy figures on the dark landing.

"Yes?"

"Mr. Will Baxter?" The voice was pleasant, but as cold as chilled steel.

Baxter nodded.

"Knowles sent us," the voice added.

Baxter opened the door. "Come in," he invited, relief softening his voice. "Come right in."

The two strangers crowded into the office. They were of a height, both standing slightly over six feet. Trail-tough men, narrow through the hips and belly—men used to riding. Lamplight glittered brashly from wide, cartridge-looped belts.

They glanced at Myers and Gates with careless interest, then at Baxter. The first man smiled. "I'm Bob Striker. This is my brother, Les."

Baxter rubbed his hands together. "Glad you

got here," he said. "Meet Reb Myers over there—and Lee Gates." He added meaningfully, "We're going to see a lot of each other from now on. Let's have a drink on it."

CHAPTER VIII

The windstorm blew itself out during the night. A high thin cloud layer filtered the early morning sun as Lou came down into the lobby. He stopped by the desk and waited a few moments, then, seeing no one, tapped the counter bell.

He heard movement behind the closed door of what was obviously Kathy Hastings' sleeping quarters, and a man's muted voice reached him. Then Kathy opened the door and came to the desk. Winters glanced past her just as the door closed; he had a glimpse of George Asher and was surprised.

Apparently the marshal was not too happy at home. . . .

He settled his hotel and stable bill with the girl and was pocketing his change when Kathy asked him if he wanted the package he had in her safe.

Lou considered briefly. He shook his head. "Keep it for me. I'll be by for it some day."

Kathy seemed under some tension. Her voice had a nasal unpleasantness as she asked: "Are you staying in the valley?"

"I'm thinking about it," Lou answered. "I've been offered a job." He nodded goodbye, picked up his warbag, and left through the side entrance leading to the stables.

Kathy leaned on her elbows and put her face in her hands. She heard the door open behind her and heard George come toward her. There was no one in the lobby. She took hold of herself and turned.

"I think he saw you," she said. Her voice was strained.

Asher shrugged. "He's only a drifter. He'll be out of the valley by night."

"No. He's staying. He said he had a job."

The marshal frowned. "With Will Baxter?"

"He didn't say." Petty hate formed little lines around her mouth. "Possibly with that Snow woman." She sniffed. "Spending time in a man's room at night—and her husband barely settled in his grave!"

George laid a hand gently on her arm. "We're in no position to cast stones, Kathy." He put his hat on his head, shoving it back as was his habit. He looked young, very boyish, but there was a sad look in his eyes.

She jerked her arm away. "It's not the same with us!" she flared. "Mary's not been your wife for months now!"

He interrupted coldly: "Let's not talk about Mary."

"Why not?" Kathy's voice rose angrily, shrilly. "How do you think I feel—seeing you for a few minutes at a time, snatching an occasional hour together, standing here and waiting for you to come in—and tortured every time you do! Wondering each night if she knows—and hoping she does—"

"Mary doesn't care about us!" George cut her off harshly. "She doesn't care what I do these days." Hurt misery crept into his tone. "All she can think of is what happened to her brother. All she remembers is that she was once accepted at Diamond T. Now she's the wife of a small town cop. Her brother is almost a recluse—a man who hates everyone—"

He sucked in a harsh breath. "I married her before Lord Telfors fired her brother. She wasn't the same person. She was a lively, happy girl. She was fun to be with."

Kathy shoved him away from her. "I don't want to hear about Mary!" she cried. "I don't care about her! I want you, George. I'm getting old. I'll be twenty-three next month. I'll never get out of Concho—" Tears washed her eyes. "George, do you know you've never even told me you loved me?"

The pathetic appeal in her voice shocked him. In the morning light she stood tall and thin and oddly unfeminine. Her smile had always been Kathy's one good point. Without it she seemed a different person—older and terribly lonely and without pride.

He felt a sudden rush of sympathy, and reached out to take her in his arms. Then he heard the heavy tread of someone coming down into the lobby and swung around the desk instead. His voice, as he stood in front of the counter, was as matter-of-fact as he could manage.

"I'll take two of my favorite cigars, Kathy."

Kathy turned blindly and reached for the cigars in the box on the shelf. She tossed them on the counter and fled into the back room.

The man who came down into the lobby glanced curiously at the marshal, nodded his greeting.

George Asher felt miserable.

Lou Winters saddled his roan and rode out between the still palms guarding the hotel gate. It was still too early to meet Louella Snow, but he was anxious to get riding. He wanted to get settled at Rainbow.

Sentinel Butte rose above the building line, a landmark plainly visible from any corner of Concho Valley. Less than sixty miles south, as the crow flies, was the Mexican border.

It could be, Lou speculated, that Ace Doolin, tired of hiding out in Mexico, had come back across the invisible line between the countries.

It could be . . . but there was a hard core of distrust in Lou. The war years had left a streak of skepticism in him. He and Frank had shared this, although Frank was by nature more outgoing.

Well, Frank Santree was dead, hanged by

Diamond T as a rustler. A sour taste came to Lou as he remembered this.

He owed Frank something. Doolin could wait. His left hand slid down over the smooth walnut butt of his Colt. What was between him and Doolin was inevitable, yet he had little taste for it.

He dismounted in front of POP HOLLAND'S CAFÉ and tied up. Glancing up from the bar, he saw a rider lope past. Surprise pinned a frown between his eyes. The grizzled old bum he had taken for the town loafer last night in Tom's Bar was slouched in the saddle of a chunky grulla. Now he didn't seem quite so old as he rode past.

He glanced at Lou, then ducked his head, and Winters thought with sharp suspicion: *Wonder who you'll be reporting to?*

His mind supplied an answer to the nagging thought, but he discarded it. Except for Farley, the small rancher who had been Luke's neighbor, he had found no one who really believed Doolin was in Concho Valley.

He turned and went into the café. A bell jingled somewhere inside the kitchen. The air was thick and blue with cigaret smoke and redolent of fried ham. Lou paused and looked over the room. The counter stools were all taken, and so were several of the half-dozen oilcloth-covered tables.

He found an unoccupied table by the wall,

under a coat rack. The cardboard sign on the wall next to it read:

IF YOU LIKE OUR FOOD SAY SO
IF YOU DON'T, SHUT UP!

Lou hung his hat on the hook and sat down. A fourteen-year-old girl with long taffy-colored hair tied with a ribbon on her neck came to take his order. Pop was busy serving the customers at the counter.

He gave his order and settled back. The men in the place gave him only cursory attention. There was subdued talk about the hangings, and one portly gent, sitting with one heavy haunch on a stool, kept insisting to his frowning companion that the Governor should be informed.

The young waitress came back with a mug of coffee for Lou and returned to the kitchen. Lou spooned sugar into his cup and stirred idly. . . . He listened with half an ear to the stout man's anger-laced argument.

"Sure we're a long way from the law, Ted! But when a man like Charley Mizner and a spoiled girl who ought to be shipped back to her father's country take upon themselves the roles of judge, jury and executioner, then it's time we thought of doing something about it!"

The man with him, tall and slope-shouldered, had the air of a harried farmer. He glanced around the room with a worried look and his voice dropped below that of his companion, as though he were afraid of being overheard.

The heavy man turned and stared at Lou, his jaw jutting challengingly.

"I'll be hanged if I will!" he said angrily. "I won't keep quiet just because some gunslinger—"

His companion got up, and the fat man subsided, grumbling, pulling him back down on the stool.

Lou smiled bleakly. Then his attention swung to the door as the bell jingled above the murmuring in the room.

Will Baxter walked in first. He looked erect and natty in his pressed black suit, and the flat-crowned black hat was set squarely on his head. He had a smile on his face, and his eyes glittered defiantly as he searched the room.

The others filed in quietly, four of them. Gates and Myers first, then the Striker brothers. The last two halted by the door, and Bob Striker took a broom straw out of his shirt pocket and began probing his teeth.

Conversation faded into uneasy silence. The clink of tableware was plainly audible; two men pushed aside unfinished plates and decided to leave.

Baxter found Lou. He swung around and came toward Winters, his smile hanging on his lips like an ornament.

Lou eased his chair back, giving his hand room. Baxter halted, and his smile changed into a challenging sneer.

"I've been looking for you, Winters!"

"You found me!" Lou's voice was blunt.

Baxter glanced at Myers, who had tagged at his heels. He looked back to Lou, bolstered by the tough kid behind him.

"You remember our talk last night?"

"Vaguely."

Baxter's eyes narrowed. "I thought I put things plain—" He pushed the rancor out of his voice, evidently deciding to be friendly.

"Look, Winters—I can use you. You don't love Diamond T. Why not throw in with me?"

Lou put his sober glance on the man behind Baxter. There was a tough, impatient look in Myers' eyes. Gates was standing farther back, showing his disinterest by reading the sign by the coat rack. The Striker brothers were watching with casual disinterest.

"Come on," Baxter urged. "What do you say, Winters?"

"I told you," Lou answered flatly. "I don't hire my gun."

"That your answer?" Baxter's voice held a snarl.

Lou nodded. "Final." He reached for his coffee cup, lifted it to his lips.

Baxter stepped back. Myers shoved past him.

The table edge pressed against his thighs as he put his palms flat on the table and shoved his hard face toward Lou.

"Mr. Baxter gave you a choice, fella! You work for him—or get out of the valley!" He sneered. "Personally, I don't like you, Winters. I'm not giving you any choice at all! Just get up and get out of here—right now!"

Lou's weight shifted slowly. Baxter was moving back, his smile fixed on his scarred face. He had set the stage, but he wasn't quite sure how the play would come off.

Lou's voice reached him with a cold warning: "Call this young pup off, Baxter, before I hurt him!"

Myers' eyes flared; blood reddened the back of his thick neck. "Hurt me?" His voice was suddenly thick. "Why, you darn fool—"

Lou swept his right hand across the table, knocking Myers' hands away. Deprived of their support, Myers' face came down hard on the table. Lou hammered him hard behind the right ear, driving his face down again; then he stood up, shoving the table over on top of Myers!

Gates waited just a moment too long. When he moved he found himself looking into Lou's Colt muzzle. He lifted both hands, his smile underlining his sudden pacifistic turn of mind.

The two gunmen by the door made no move. They had not expected to take a hand in what had been intended to be nothing more than a scare thrown into a stranger.

Myers was on the floor. Blood streamed from his flattened nose, making a mess of his shirt. He fumbled for his Colt, slid it free, and Lou stepped down hard on his knuckles. Myers cried out and let go of the Colt. Lou kicked it under the table.

Still holding his gun in his left hand, he reached down and yanked Myers to his feet. The blond kid twisted free and swung wildly for Lou's face. Winters stepped aside, then came close and slapped Myers' face hard, sending him reeling against Baxter.

Myers was sobbing with senseless rage. He staggered away from Baxter and pawed at his face and managed to get blood into his eyes.

Lou said wickedly: "Get him out of here, Baxter!"

Baxter's face was drawn tight over his prominent cheekbones. Behind him Bob Striker stirred. His voice held a lazy, deadly drawl.

"You want us to take him, Mr. Baxter?"

It was Gates who answered him. "Not now, Bob." He looked at Lou. "You shouldn't have done this, fella. Not to Myers."

Lou sneered.

Baxter finally mustered his voice. "I gave you a choice!" he said savagely. "But after this—"

Myers focused his gaze enough to locate Lou.

He uttered a strangled sound and lunged for Winters.

Lou stepped aside and Myers slammed into the wall, bounced back and remembered his other Colt. His hand was reaching for it when Lou laid the side of his own Colt across Myers' head.

The man fell across the overturned table.

Lou pushed his shoulders back against the wall. There was a bright deadly anger in his eyes, a bleak and chilling smile on his lips.

"I'm giving you no choice at all, Baxter!" he snapped. "Get that tough kid out of here—and stay out of my way!"

Baxter's temper chilled. He sucked in a slow breath, nodded. He turned to the Striker boys. "Get him out!"

They walked up to Myers' limp figure. Bob Striker reached down, hooked his fingers under Myers' arms and lifted the man clear of the floor. His brother ducked a shoulder under the sagging figure, and they went out.

Baxter turned at the door. He had the last word.

"I said no one sits on the fence in Concho Valley. You had your chance, Winters! You'll live just long enough to regret your choice!"

The room seemed suddenly full of noise. Men started eating, clinking crockery and tableware. The girl came toward Lou as he was righting the table; she waited while he smoothed the tablecloth over it, then set his breakfast plate in front of him. She went back into the kitchen for a dustpan and broom to sweep up the broken cup and sugar bowl. . . .

The florid-faced man slid off his stool and came to Lou's table. He hooked a thumb in his vest pocket, just above a heavy gold chain with the emblem of the Elks dangling from it.

"I'm Paul Stockton," he introduced himself. "Stockton Freight Line."

Lou gave him a glance, then went on eating.

The man was thick-skinned. "I like your style, feller," he continued. "I think you're the man Concho needs." He pulled a chair up to the table and sat down, facing Lou. "Between Will Baxter and the Diamond T, a decent peaceful man can't earn a living any more."

Lou looked at him. "You look like you're doing fine," he said.

Paul Stockton flushed. "I'll keep on doing fine!" he snapped. "But I'm thinking of the rest of the folks in the valley. If someone doesn't curb that fool Baxter he'll get us all involved in his trouble with Diamond T."

Lou was conscious that most of the diners were looking at them. He shrugged. "None of my business," he said flatly.

"It could be." Stockton's tone held a flat confidence. "At three hundred a month, say?"

Lou looked up, annoyance crowding the

patience from his gray eyes. “Whose side are you on?”

“All the peaceful folk in the valley,” Stockton replied. He leaned forward over the table. “I saw how you handled that gunman Baxter brought in. Quick, clean. And the way you drew! I haven’t seen a smoother, faster—”

“Thanks,” Lou cut in abruptly.

“This town needs a lawman,” Stockton said sharply. “A man who’ll—”

“You have one,” Lou pointed out.

“George?” Stockton’s heavy jowls shook. “Baxter’s brother-in-law? He’s all right when he’s handling drunks. But he wags his tail every time Will throws him a bone.” Stockton shook his head. “I’m head of the town council, Mr. Winters. You take over George’s job and see that Baxter’s men stay clear of town. The same with Diamond T. I don’t care what they do to each other—as long as they stay clear of Concho.”

Lou looked him over carefully. “You don’t really want peace, do you?” His voice was flat, cynical. “Will Baxter’s got a grudge against Diamond T and hires gunmen for a showdown. Diamond T’s having trouble with rustlers, so they lynch two honest men. You run a freight line. All you’re interested in is seeing that a shooting war doesn’t break out in town.”

He put a palm against Stockton’s chest and

shoved. "Get out of my way, Stockton. You're spoiling my breakfast."

The freight line owner rose, his face congested. "You two-bit gunman! I offered you an honest job. Now I'm taking it back. And I'll see that you and your kind are run out of Concho—"

Lou made a motion as if he were getting up. Stockton backed away, whirled and went out, slamming the door.

No one bothered Winters for the rest of his meal.

CHAPTER IX

Louella Snow was waiting impatiently in the buggy when Lou rode up. Reverend and Amy Stone were by the gate, saying goodbye.

The Reverend's voice held sharp reproof as Lou drew close.

"No one ever benefited by hate, Louella. What Diamond T did was wrong—terribly wrong. But hating Nina Telfors isn't going to bring Luke back. Nor hiring a gunman."

"I'm sorry, Reverend," Louella said. There was a blunt impatience in her voice. "I'm not like you. When I'm hurt I want to hit back. When someone hurts me the way Nina Telfors did, I hate!"

Reverend Stone made a weary gesture. "What will all this gain you? What do you hope to accomplish by staying on at Rainbow. It's no place for a woman alone—"

"It's home," she said sharply. "Rainbow represents my stake in the valley." She smiled without much warmth. "See it as a matter of pride, Reverend. Nina Telfors wants me to leave. I'm going to stay."

Reverend Stone nodded, his gesture resigned. "As you wish, Louella. But I want you to know that I'm going to the Governor. You see, it's more than your hate, and Will Baxter's, which is at stake here. Diamond T has made a lot of enemies. Lord Telfors was a tyrant, and his daughter, unfortunately, hasn't helped change the animosity her father created. Will Baxter has his personal reasons for hating her, and so have you." And, his glance lifted to Lou sitting silently in saddle alongside the buggy, "So has Mr. Winters. But an all-out war against Diamond T will not really settle anything. If you could only see this—both of you!"

"Diamond T didn't care when they hanged my husband. And you forget the passage in the Bible, Reverend, which says something about an eye for an eye. . . ."

"We have outgrown the old Mosaic Law," Stone said. He shook his head. "There is another passage which speaks of turning the other cheek."

"I can't," Louella said. She leaned forward, her smile softening. "I'm sorry, Reverend. You've been very kind. You and Mrs. Stone have been the only friends I've made here. I want to thank you for everything you've done for me."

She sat back and lightly slapped the animal with the loose end of her reins. Amy waved. Lou nodded briefly and followed the buggy. They swung onto Main Street and turned out of town.

They rode past Baxter's office. Gates had just come down the long flight of outside stairs and was standing on the walk, lighting a cigaret. He straightened as they rode by, and Lou kept an alert glance on him.

George Asher came out of his small office farther on. He waved an arm and called out something, but Lou ignored him. He kept alongside the buggy, and when they hit the downslope out of town Louella turned and eyed him with sharp reproof.

"You were late," she said. "What kept you?"

"A little trouble," he answered shortly. He didn't like her tone, and he let his roan fall slightly behind and to one side of the buggy. She looked back, her lips tightening. But she kept her annoyance bottled up.

They left Concho behind them, keeping in the early morning shadow of Sentinel Butte. The air was deceptively clear. The far hills were deep blue in shadow, the peaks stark with the morning sun on them.

Concho Valley opened up as they swung away from the butte, tilted slightly, like a rough-edged platter. The slope of the land fell away to the southwest, toward low, desolate sandstone hills that hid a hundred waterless canyons.

Rainbow was on the Quicksilver. The creek came out of the high, scantily timbered country north of Concho Valley. It went dry every summer, but it retained enough surface water in scattered, cottonwood-shaded pools to see a small ranch through the dry season.

Rainbow's nearest neighbor was Horace Farley, six miles down on the Quicksilver.

They reached Rainbow at noon. The sun was hot over the land. A rooster crowed lustily by the corral fence and beat his chest with his wings.

A one-armed man in pants and wool underwear came out of the barn to take care of the buggy. He was a long, wrinkled, untidy man who could have been thirty—or sixty.

Louella said: "I'll make dinner. You and Pete can get acquainted." Her voice was civil, reserved.

She went into the house. Pete took the gelding into the barn. As far as he was concerned, he was not about to be friendly. Lou shrugged. He led the roan to the trough by the corral, pumped water into it and let the animal drink. While he waited he glanced around the spread.

There were flower beds around the house, which seemed solidly and carefully built of heavy timbers. It wasn't big. It had two chimneys, one obviously a fireplace. The front porch was deep, with a wider overhang. From one of the wicker chairs on it a man could see across the creek, far up a desolate, mysterious canyon beyond.

It had an air of deep peace about it.

Lou unsaddled and turned the roan into the corral. A long-legged gray mare came over, muzzling the roan. Lou recognized the animal as Frank's mount.

Pete was already at the table when he entered

the kitchen. It was a small ell, separated from the main house by a covered breezeway. Honeysuckle screened the open sides.

Louella had discarded the black dress. She had replaced it with a plain gingham, and put on an apron.

There was little conversation during the plain meal. Lou asked about the ranch and how many cattle it stocked. Louella got up and went to the house and returned with a tally book and handed it to Winters.

Luke's handwriting was small and precise. Looking at the entries Lou shaped a picture of Luke. A meticulous man, a careful man. It didn't altogether fit with what Louella had told him about a dreamer, a man who could name a ranch Rainbow.

What had Luke known about Nina Telfors that she would have wanted him killed? What did this woman across the table know?

He closed the book. "According to these figures you should have about seventy-two head. I didn't see one on the way in."

"They're in a small valley back of us," Louella said. "Herefords. Some Whitefaces. Luke was experimenting with cross-breeding. I don't know much about cattle, Mr. Winters, but I'm going to learn."

He got up. "I might as well start earning my keep. I'll take a look around—"

"You'll have to bunk with Pete," Louella said.

"Ain't no room for him!" Pete said. He was as belligerent as a scrawny-necked rooster. He got up and glared at Louella. "You didn't tell me you was bringing help back with you. Don't need help. I kin handle what work there is around the place."

"You'll keep doing your work," Louella said. Her voice was firm. "Mr. Winters will take care of his own chores."

She smiled as Pete snorted and stomped out.

Lou grinned. "Cranky old cuss, ain't he?"

"Pete's like one of the family," she said. Her voice was cold; he sensed a desire to keep a distance between them. She started collecting the dishes. "Pete was an old Diamond T hand—one of the few hands who remained with Diamond T when John Spender sold out to Lord Telfors. Telfors fired him when a horse he was breaking pinned him against the corral bars. The doctor had to amputate his arm."

"Fired?"

She looked at him with level gaze. "Lord Telfors had no use for a man or an animal who couldn't give him a day's work. So Luke told me. When we came back to Concho Valley and settled here, Luke hired Pete, who was hanging around town, living off crumbs. We couldn't afford it then, but Luke never let Pete know. Luke gave him chores he could have done himself; he made Pete feel he was earning his wages."

Winters said quietly, "I think I would have liked Luke."

"Everyone did, except Nina Telfors . . ." She turned away, carrying the dishes to the sink. He hesitated a moment, eyeing her slim figure. There was a barrier between them—one Louella had raised.

He turned and left the kitchen.

Pete was standing by a sawbuck, a cedar-handled bucksaw leaning against his shanks. He was stuffing tobacco into a corncob pipe, holding the pipe deftly under the stump of his left arm.

Lou met the man's fierce stare. "Where do you bunk?"

Pete took his time answering. He looked Lou over from head to toe; his wind-creased neck was stiff. "In there." He jerked his unshaven jaw to the shed behind him.

Lou walked past him and looked into the shed. One section was walled off with odd scraps of lumber. He could see through the wide cracks, and judged there was little room for more than a bunk inside.

He turned away, conscious of Pete's unfriendly regard. He went into the barn, which was big enough to have a loft. A couple of chickens ran out as he went in.

The buggy was in one corner. A few sacks of grain were piled in the other, and there was a neat row of hen's nests along the back wall. Harness was hung on woodpegs along the walls. There was a ladder leading up to the loft.

He climbed the ladder and stood on the upper rungs, surveying the space under the slanting roof. A small window level with the floor gave him a view of the yard and the trail. . . . Lou accepted this as better than sleeping out in the open or moving in with Pete.

He came down and fetched his warbag and brought it up to the loft. Pete was sawing, his corncob clenched between stubby teeth, when he came out of the barn.

He made himself a smoke, conserving the few cigars he had left. Pete sawed steadily. He was a lean, whipcord-framed man. He cut through the twelve-inch log and laid the saw against the horse and wiped sweat from his brow.

Lou said: "There's going to be trouble, Pete. That's why I'm here."

The turkey-necked man looked at him. He had young blue eyes under shaggy eyebrows. "Trouble's already happened," he grunted. A futile anger glinted in his eyes.

"It's just started," Lou said. He looked toward the house. "As long as she stays on at Rainbow, Diamond T's going to make trouble."

Pete took the corncob from his pants pocket.

"I got a twelve-gauge shotgun in the shed," he said calmly. He looked at Lou questioningly with narrow eyes.

"You look like the jaspers who ride for Diamond T. How come yo're working for Mrs. Snow?"

"Frank Santree was my partner."

Pete absorbed this bit of information. "Friend of Luke's?"

"Never met him," Lou answered. "Frank knew him. We were headed for Salinas, but Frank remembered Luke was in Concho Valley. He left me at Wild Horse Gulch, took the fork to the valley. I went on to Salinas. When he didn't show up I came looking for him."

Pete took the unlighted pipe from his mouth. "What did you say yore name was?"

"Lou Winters."

Pete stuffed the pipe back into his pocket. He held out his hand. "Glad yo're here, Lou."

They shook. Pete glanced at the house. "They'll come again," he said grimly. "They wanted Luke out of the way. Now they'll come for her."

Lou frowned. "Why, Pete? What has Diamond T got against Rainbow?"

The older man shrugged. "Something Luke knew about Nina Telfors, something he told Mrs. Snow. I don't know what it is. But Diamond T kept after Luke. A half-dozen times they tried to force him into a gunfight. Luke wouldn't fight."

"Sometimes it's harder not to fight," Lou murmured.

Pete nodded. "Luke wasn't afraid. But he knew what they were after. And he knew he didn't stand a chance against Diamond T's gunhands. I reckon he was thinking of her, too—"

Lou took a long breath. "So they finally got him on a rustling charge? Frank, too?"

"Frank didn't matter," Pete said thinly. "He just happened to get here at the wrong time." He frowned, cocked his head to one side. "You looking for this Doolin longrider, too?"

"That's why I went to Salinas," Lou said.

"Frank was looking for Doolin. I heard him talking with Luke. He seemed plumb surprised at the talk that Doolin was hiding out in the back hills here."

Lou stiffened. "I'm surprised, too. Is Doolin in the Tombstones?"

"No." Pete's voice was harsh. "Charley Mizner's been stealing Diamond T blind. He was smart enough to know he'd have to have a goat when the losses showed in the tally book. So he picked the first name he saw on a dodger. It happened to be Ace Doolin."

Lou dropped his butt and ground it to shreds under his heel. "You sure of this, old-timer?"

"Dead sure." Pete brushed the back of his hand across his lips. "Luke knew what Charley was doing. But he wasn't really sure Doolin wasn't in the hills. When Frank showed up and said Doolin was in Mexico, Luke decided to see Nina Telfors. He didn't tell Mrs. Snow. But I heard him and Frank talking. Luke was sorry for the Telfors girl. He didn't hold anything against her." Pete turned and spit into the sawdust under the horse. "Luke was funny that way. He couldn't get mad at anybody."

"Then Luke and Frank might have been hanged because they knew about Doolin," Lou said softly. "It might have been Charley Mizner's idea all along—not the Telfors girl's."

Pete glanced at the house. "Don't tell her about it," he muttered. "She's plumb convinced the Telfors girl killed Luke."

"You were here when they brought Frank and Luke back?"

Pete nodded. "I was in the shed when they rode up. Sam Keeler held a gun on me while the others dumped Luke and Frank out of the wagon. They had their cayuses tied to the tailgate. They turned them loose in the yard. Charley was driving. He waited until Mrs. Snow came to the door. Then he told her about catching Luke and Frank red-handed, and something about her knowing Nina Telfors' orders."

Lou pushed his hat back on his head. "Real neighborly folks," he muttered. He was thinking that both Charley Mizner and the Telfors girl had had reasons for killing Luke.

“Where’s Farley’s spread?” he asked.

Pete pointed. “Just south of that rock jut. ’Bout six miles.”

“I met Farley last night,” Lou said. “Sat in a poker game with him and a farmer named Gillian—”

Pete snorted, showing what he thought of both men.

“Farley seemed sure Doolin was in the country. He said his man saw Doolin leaving Rainbow.”

Pete grinned. “Slim’s got a powerful ’magination. He must have seen the same dodger Charley Mizner did.”

Lou nodded soberly. “See what you mean, Pete.” He headed for the corral. “I’ll saddle Frank’s gray and take a look around. See you at suppertime.”

Pete watched him saddle the frisky mare, wheel away. A thought came to nag him. “Wonder what he and Frank wanted with Doolin?” he muttered. . . .

CHAPTER X

The small campfire did not show above the jumbled rocks. But Gip Upson smelled it. He swung his horse in that direction, threading a way through the rocks, and finally hit the old trail he had been looking for.

A few minutes later he came to the clearing where an old mine shaft, its timbers caved, peered down from a rust-streaked slope. A still discernible footpath led from a sagging, broken-windowed shack to the mine, mute testimony to the perseverance of the miner who had worked it.

The rifle guard on the rock at the head of the clearing waved him on. Gip slouched further down in the saddle and scratched an irritation on his hairy ear.

He was the bum Lou Winters had bought beer for in Tom's Bar . . . the seemingly senile oldster who had been whittling a ship in the saloon when Lou first saw him.

Four men were playing poker around an old blanket. One man was sprawled on his back, asleep by the small spring back of the shack.

A rangy, blue-eyed man was sitting on an old dynamite box in front of an easel. A Remington .44 jutted from a worn black leather holster. He was making swift marks with a piece of charcoal on the board on the easel.

He heard Upson's horse and got to his feet. A cigaret dangled from his lips, giving his face a careless look.

This man was Ace Doolin.

Upson swung his tired bronc over to the outlaw boss and stepped stiffly down from the saddle. The others quit their poker playing and came toward them.

"Danged hot ride," Upson complained. "Forgot to take a canteen with me."

Doolin said sharply, "Get him some water, Jake!" He took a slim black cigar from his pocket and handed it to Upson. "How'd you make out?"

Upson shrugged. "I found out what we want to know. The bank's a cinch. Won't be much of a haul, but we'll have no trouble getting it."

"How much law in town?"

"Only a younker by name of Asher." Upson worked his tongue across dry lips and spat out grit. "Shoot a gun off near his ear and he won't stop running."

Jake came back with a canteen, and Upson tilted it to his lips. His Adam's apple bobbed appreciatively.

Doolin tossed his piece of charcoal aside. "Reckon we've been loafing long enough, boys. Time we picked up some easy money and ducked back across the border."

Upson lowered the canteen and corked it.

"I found out something else, Ace—something you'll be interested in."

Doolin gave him a searching look.

"There was a hombre in town, asking for you," Upson said. He smirked. "Right sociable cuss—bought me a coupla bottles of beer."

Ace frowned. "Law?"

"He wasn't wearing a badge," Upson said. "Had yore kind of build, only his hair was dark. And he was fast, Ace—real fast. Saw him tangle with a couple of tough gunhawks from the big spread in the valley, Diamond T." He chuckled. "They buried one of them. . . ."

Doolin was growing impatient. "All right—so you met a fast gun asking for me. What did he want?"

"Near as I could make out, he came to town looking for his partner, a gent named Frank Santree."

Doolin started. Upson paused, stared at him.

"Frank Santree? You sure of that name?" Doolin's voice had an edge to it.

"That's the name I heard," Upson muttered.

Doolin sighed. The years slipped by in memory. He saw a dusty road leading across an old cornfield. He saw three weary cavalrymen, temporarily cut off from their regiment, pause by an old mill pond, shuck their clothes and splash happily, like kids, while war moved past them, heading south.

He bent and picked up the piece of charcoal and turned to the board where he had been sketching the mine shaft on the slope. With a few deft strokes he outlined a round face, indicated a short pug nose, laughing eyes.

"That was Frank," he said.

Upson frowned. "Didn't see him," he muttered. His voice held a dry sarcasm. "Diamond T hands hung him the day I got to town!"

Doolin stiffened. But he didn't turn around. He drew another face—longer, harder. The eyes were unsmiling.

"The man who asked about me—Frank's partner—did he look like this?"

Upson squinted at the charcoal sketch. "Yeah. That's him."

Doolin's lips held an odd regret. "Lou Winters."

"That's the name he signed on the hotel register," Upson said. "You know him?"

Doolin nodded. "I knew Frank Santree, too."

Upson was curious. The others were waiting to hear what Doolin had to say. They were a ragged lot, men who had stepped across the line of no return as far as the law was concerned. Each man was heavily armed, and no one thought further than the present. No man made long-range plans; for them the future always hung on the business end of a gun.

Doolin looked them over; his glance went past them to the hot slopes ringing the clearing.

Of the three his had seemed the most promising future. But he had wound up here, a man with a price on his head, leading a bunch of cut-throats. . . .

Upson broke in on his thoughts. "I found out a few other things, Ace. Ran into dodgers all over the valley and in town. Diamond T claims we've been raiding them for months. They've got a pretty good description of you from one of the old North Platte dodgers—"

Doolin cut in coldly. "What in the devil are you talking about? We've only been here three days!"

"We know that," Upson said, "but the valley don't." He knuckled his grizzled jaw. "Somebody at Diamond T's been using you as a cover for a double-cross. Looks like someone's raiding Diamond T beef, and we're the goats. To make it look good they hung a small rancher named Luke Snow and this Frank Santree. Claimed they caught them red-handed, stealing Diamond T beef. Even claimed they were Ace Doolin riders!"

Jake, a squat, burly character, grumbled: "Might be smart if we forgot that bank, Ace. If the whole valley's already on the lookout for us—"

"We'll let them find us!" Ace snapped. Malice glittered in his eyes. "So Diamond T's using me as their goat? Hung Frank as one of my riders?" His laughter had a bitter edge. "Only Frank could know how much of a joke that was."

Upson was blunt. "What are we going to do about the bank?"

"We'll bust it wide open," Doolin snapped, "in due time. But first we'll give Diamond T a taste of their own medicine."

"What about this hombre Winters?"

"What about him?" Doolin demanded harshly.

Upson made a quick gesture. "He was looking for you. Seemed to me he wanted you real bad."

Doolin's eyes lidded. "I'll let him find me, Gip."

Horace Farley came to the door when he heard the rider. He stepped out to the sagging porch and shaded his eyes against the slanting sun. He had a moment of quick hope; then, when he recognized the rangy figure on the gray mare, a hostile frown settled over his narrow face.

He waited until Lou Winters drew up before the porch.

Lou nodded. "Howdy." He glanced around at the ramshackle spread. Farley had a little truck garden along the creek and he had seeded an acre of oats, but he seemed a poor farmer. There was a hog pen under some cottonwoods. But Farley, a bachelor, did not seem happy ranching—and Lou guessed shrewdly that Farley was the kind of man who would never be happy doing anything.

"Sort of wandered off the main trail, haven't you?" Farley asked. His tone was unfriendly, but not hostile; there was an uneasy curiosity in him as to what had brought Winters out there.

"Just taking a look around," Lou answered. "I'm working for Rainbow."

Farley's eyes flickered. "Didn't know Louella planned to stay on." He put his gaze on Lou's holstered gun. "Didn't know she had the money to hire gunfighters, either."

"Might be there's a lot about your neighbor you don't know," Lou said. He leaned on his forearms. "Mind if I come in? Horse could stand a drink and so could I."

Farley hesitated. His attention flickered to the slim youngster who stood in the barn doorway. He was a gangling man of twenty with an untidy mop of sandy hair.

"Sure, come in," Farley invited. But his tone held a grudging reluctance. He called out to the youngster, "Slim, take care of Mr. Winters' mare. . . ."

Lou followed him inside. The ranchhouse was a bit like Farley; it had an untidy, nervous look.

"I don't keep liquor in the house," Farley apologized. "Got some ginger beer, if you care for it—"

Lou smiled. "Haven't tasted the stuff since I was a boy. Sure would like to try it again, Farley."

"Name's Horace," Farley said gruffly. He waved Lou to a chair and went out the back door.

Lou looked over the big room. There was a small tintype of a man and a woman and a boy, obviously Horace and his parents, on a walnut table by the window. There was a soiled gray flannel shirt tossed over a saggy-bottomed sofa. The cat lying under the stove was a battle-scarred tom, and he twitched nervously in his sleep.

Lou thought back to the conversation he had heard last night. Farley had seemed disappointed when he'd ridden up. Had he been expecting someone else? Nina Telfors? He had been kidded about the Diamond T girl by his companions.

How much truth was there to that story? Obviously enough to nettle Farley.

Lou found himself becoming keenly interested in finding out what kind of a woman Nina Telfors was.

He was rolling a cigaret when Farley came back with a quart bottle. He uncorked it with a loud popping noise, and some of the ginger beer spumed out. . . . He thrust his palm over it until he could get it to the glasses on the sink.

"Made it myself," he said, handing a glass to Lou. "Easier on the stomach than Tom's beer."

Lou took a sip of it and found it better than he had anticipated. He took a long swallow.

"I've been checking on Rainbow's stock," he explained. "I understand Luke owned about seventy-two head: some Whitefaces, the rest Herefords. I counted about twenty Whitefaces;

didn't see a Hereford with the Rainbow brand on it."

Farley frowned. "Rainbow's beef never drifts this way. If they drift at all they move north, up in the canyons that Diamond T claims." He finished his ginger beer and rolled the glass between his palms. "Copper Springs line shack is up that way. Diamond T keeps a man up there all year long."

Lou caught the veiled suggestion. "Reckon I'll ask him," he said.

Farley's smile held a malicious twist. "Better see him first, before you ride up. All Diamond T hands are under orders to shoot first at strangers—"

"So I heard," Lou cut in. His voice held bleak amusement. "Diamond T ever bother you?"

Farley shook his head. "Nor anyone else around here. Ned Gillian farms a section with his brother down below here. He's never been bothered. Joe Hooker has a place north—I never heard him complain. There's Baker's B-in-the-Box way west—Baker never had trouble with Diamond T."

Lou was puzzled. "What about Luke Snow?"

Farley leaned back. "I don't know about Luke. He wasn't very neighborly. I dropped by his place a couple of times. Oh, he was pleasant enough, I guess. But he seemed to like being alone up there on the Rainbow."

"Had he had trouble with Rainbow before?"

"Nina—Miss Telfors didn't like him. She didn't trust him, she said."

"You know Miss Telfors pretty well?" Lou's voice was gently prodding.

Farley's neck reddened. He seemed suddenly to realize he had talked too much, gabbled on like some garrulous lonely man, which he was.

"I see her sometimes," he muttered. "She rides around alone a lot since her father died."

Lou took another tack. "I just hired on at Rainbow," he said. "I kinda want to know what I'm getting into."

"Trouble," Farley growled. "I think Luke was tied up with that Doolin gang for a long time, even before he quit Diamond T. He made a mistake when he let that Doolin longrider they caught with him visit him."

"You're sure about this Doolin?" Lou said. He put a touch of apprehension in his voice.

"Heck, I know what you heard last night," Farley said, rising to the bait. "But them danged fools let their hate of Diamond T blind them to the real trouble here. Some day, after that Doolin gang busts the town wide open, they'll see their mistake."

"You said your puncher saw Doolin?" Lou probed.

Farley got to his feet. "Ask him yoreself," he growled. He walked to the door, called to Slim.

The puncher came in, ducking to clear the door.

He was very tall and thin and his hands seemed to brush his bony knees.

"Slim—this is Lou Winters. He just hired on at Rainbow."

Slim bobbed his head. "Howdy."

"He wants to know where you saw Ace Doolin."

Slim stared. Then he knuckled his shovel jaw embarrassedly. "Saw him over by Rainbow," he muttered. "He and a coupla other jaspers were crossing the Quicksilver over by Coffin Point."

"When?"

"The night before Luke and that friend of his were caught by Diamond T and hung."

"You sure it was Doolin," Lou asked sharply, "not just someone you thought was him?"

Slim's high brow creased. "I recognized him. The moon was out. I was coming back from town and stopped to let my bronc blow. I heard riders; then I saw these three strangers come across the creek. No water there now. They stopped and said something, and one of them rode away. He looked like an old fellow; he rode a grulla. But Doolin and the other feller turned back and headed toward Rainbow—"

"What did Doolin look like?"

"Rangy feller, built a little like you," Slim said. "Had light hair, wore a black leather cartridge belt and one gun. And he did a funny thing."

Slim looked at Farley. The rancher shrugged.

"He took a pack of cards out of his pocket," Slim said. His voice held a thin, stubborn note of defiance. "I saw him pick one out, throw it over his shoulder. After they had gone I went over and picked it up." He reached in his pocket and handed Lou a card.

It was the ace of spades.

Little ridges rose on Lou's jaw. Very few men knew of Herb Dolan's, alias Ace Doolin's superstitious gesture. In the war years they had been together, just before a dangerous mission, Herb Dolan had always taken the ace of spades out of the pack he carried and tossed it away.

Lou finished his ginger beer, got up. "Thanks," he told Slim. He looked at Farley. "Maybe I won't be staying on at Rainbow."

Farley walked to the door with him. "I don't think Louella Snow had anything to do with it," he said. "But Rainbow's no place for a woman alone."

"There's Pete," Lou murmured.

"Wouldn't trust him far as I kin spit!" Farley snapped. "Just a bum Luke picked up."

Lou turned away. He didn't want his displeasure to show. Farley must have known what had happened to Pete. But he was a small and narrow man living in his own world of petty frustrations.

Santree's mare was tied under the pecan tree by the corral. Lou mounted, waved briefly to Farley, and left the place.

It was mid-afternoon and curiosity drew him north, toward Copper Springs. Somewhere out in the broken country was Ace Doolin. He was sure of it now, although it didn't make sense, Ace Doolin had come back across the border. And the grizzled oldster he had seen in Tom's Bar was one of his men, sent ahead to ferret out the lay of the land in Concho.

Maybe Farley was the only man who had things straight. Lou had never known Ace Doolin to have any interest in cows. Banks were his specialty.

But if Doolin was planning to raid Concho, why was Diamond T claiming the Doolin gang was responsible for the wholesale rustling of Diamond beef?

The logical answer brought a thin smile to Lou's lips. There was only one thing certain now. Trouble was going to hit Concho Valley—and hit it hard.

CHAPTER XI

Nina Telfors threw her book across the bedroom and sat up on the brocaded chaise longue. A restless energy raced savagely within her; she twisted her sleek, sinuous body around as though turning toward some unseen, unheard caller. She raised her hands above her head and her lips parted in a soundless cry, a wild and bitter railing against the harsh goddess of fate.

The sun streamed into the big bedroom through the wide balcony window. A breeze fluttered the satin drapes, caressing them with old and experienced hands.

Another day. She flinched from the long and meaningless hours ahead, while the restless energy in her drove her to some sort of action. There were currents within her which she did not understand. She lived between extremes of emotion—between patience and uncontrolled anger—between love and hate.

She was mistress of this big house and of the vast acres adjacent to it—yet she walked with insecurity, with a terror that never left her. Not even the hanging of Luke Snow had given her ease. . . .

She got up and walked to the French windows and looked over the wrought-iron railing which guarded the balcony. The window gave her a view of rolling hills and the far high bulk of the Mogollons, white-capped and visible on clear days.

It commanded most of Diamond T's immediate domain—the buildings in which her crew ate, slept and worked when they were at the ranch.

They were adobe buildings mostly, interspersed with several wooden sheds. . . . A half-dozen Mexican laborers tilled fields beyond the corrals. Two fat stodgy Mexican women were washing clothes in the small creek while a group of small brown children splashed and played in it.

The main house was of stone: a massive, square, battlemented structure thrusting like an anachronism out of the dry Arizona earth; a misfit in a land where the habitations tended to take on the protective coloring of the baked earth, adapt themselves to the environment.

Her father had modelled it after their ancestral home in Austria. It was a lumpish structure, better fitted for the rigors of mid-European winters than for the southern Arizona climate.

She heard a slight rustling movement behind her and she knew that her maid, Juanita, had come into the room. She hated the stealthy, obsequious way the girl had. She was older than Nina, yet she walked like a child, her eyes downcast, a whipped-dog look about her.

She ignored the girl, and the girl remained

silent, waiting. There was a thin bluish bruise on Juanita's cheek where Nina had hit her with a slipper yesterday. She was wearing in her hair, a beautiful tortoise-shell comb, a gift from her mistress, also given to her yesterday in quick repentance of an anger over which Nina seemed to have no control.

Nina Telfors brought her gaze back from the far peaks. This was home, this big, lonely block of a house. And it was her prison.

And now the old, familiar voice began to cry out in her. Those men below who glanced covertly up at her window and sometimes made remarks that evoked ribald laughter—they were hard, unprincipled men. Even her father had distrusted them. They worked here for money and money alone; not one of them had any loyalty to Diamond T.

Her father must have known this and feared it, for he had told her to sell the ranch and leave Concho Valley when he realized he was dying.

But she knew she could never sell Diamond T. For there was no place for her to go!

She turned away from the window and faced the big ornate mirror over her vanity. The slim, dark-skinned girl with the big dark eyes and long raven-black hair was breathtakingly beautiful.

She eyed her reflection, posing, ignoring the silent girl by the door. And yet she bore an almost startling resemblance to that Mexican maid. The difference lay in the fire in her eyes, in the proud carriage of her body, in the quick grace of her stride.

She was Nina Telfors, (Anglicized from Telforz), only daughter and heir of Lord Telfors, who could trace his lineage back to one of the oldest houses of nobility in Austria.

She was Nina Telfors, whose mother was the stolid, ignorant Pima Indian cook in the Telfors household.

The blood line was there—and no gloss of private schooling, fine clothes and position could ever eradicate her savage ancestry.

A half-breed!

She heard a man's rough and insinuating laughter from below, and though it had no connection with her thoughts, she shrank from the window with a guilty flush.

Juanita took a few hesitant steps toward her.

Nina flung out an imperious arm. "Get Jose to saddle Temper right away! I'll be down in five minutes!"

Juanita backed away. . . .

Nina took a jacket from her clothes closet. It was of soft buckskin, with a belt which cinched it in at her waist. She came back to the dresser and ran her fingers through her black, silky hair, hating it, hating her brunette coloring.

Her father had been a big-boned, blond

man. . . . All the heroines of her childhood dreams had been blonde.

She gathered the mass of her hair in her hand and tied it with a bit of yellow silk ribbon; she picked out a big soft gray Stetson hat and fastened the holding thong loosely under her chin.

There was a gathering impatience in her to be off, to gallop wildly into the distance. She wanted to ride this wild, cruel misery off her back.

She slammed the door behind her and heard it echo emptily. Stepping out to the mahogany railing of the open balcony, she looked down into the huge hall.

Juanita was just coming in. The Mexican girl glanced up and immediately lowered her gaze. She stopped by the newel post and waited while Nina Telfors ran down the wide curving stairs, riding crop in hand.

She saw her mother come to the kitchen door. Rosa never said anything to her. She stood, as wide as she was tall, with a hint of the beauty that had been hers twenty years before.

Nina ignored her. She went out, heading across the gravel drive toward the corral.

A tall, muscular puncher turned as she came across the drive. He had been talking with Ramos, the *remuda* boss; he said something now out of the corner of his hard mouth which brought a hesitant grin to Ramos' lips. Then he thumbed his hat back on his balding head and stepped out to intercept the fast-walking girl.

He put himself in her path, touched his hat with a gesture that held more insolence than politeness.

"Charley went to town," he said. "He said for you to wait until he got back."

Nina stiffened. Since she could remember, no one, not even her father, had crossed her. And whatever these crude, tough men who rode for Diamond T had thought, they had kept their laughter and their innuendoes to themselves. No one had dared to speak roughly to her, let alone stop her from going where she wished.

Her voice rang harshly, with unquestioned authority. "Get out of my way!"

Sluice Williams laughed. "Charley gave strict orders, Miss Telfors. He said to see you stayed here at the ranch."

"Charley Mizner is my ranch manager, not my boss!" Nina flared. "You'll take my orders, not his!" She lifted her quirt in a threatening gesture. "Now get out of my way before I have you thrown off this ranch!"

He didn't move. His eyes held a slow malice. "You look right pretty when you get yore back up." He took a step toward her. "Real pretty—"

She slashed at his face with the quirt. But he was waiting for it. He caught her wrist and twisted the quirt from her hand, spinning her around and clamping his other arm around her waist.

His face was close, and she could see the reddish brown stubble of his beard, the flecks in his eyes. His arm was hard—his whole body was hard. She could smell stale tobacco on his breath and an animal odor that repelled her.

"I ain't Baxter!" he told her. "Don't ever try to use that whip on me again!"

She tore herself free, whirled. Rage brought tears to her eyes. No one would have dared lay a hand on her while her father was alive. But she was now a prisoner of the empire her father had built—chained to it by the secret link of blood.

Charley Mizner knew. And Luke had known. How many others knew, and eyed her with secret contempt?

She ran back across the drive to the house. She darted past a startled Juanita, ran up the broad curving stairs to her bedroom. She found the gun with the pearl handles, a German .32 caliber her father had given her as a birthday present.

She turned and ran back down the stairs.

Sluice Williams was standing by the corral, cupping a match to his cigaret, when the first bullet smashed into his shoulder. He twisted and fell back against the bars, his lips twisted with pain. He tried to face the girl.

The second bullet caught him in the stomach. He gasped and huddled over, shock widening his eyes. He made a tremendous effort and straightened and reached for his holstered gun, but there was only the will to kill in him and not the ability.

His neck sinews bulged. “You wild . . .”

Nina’s third bullet hit him in the face, just above the bridge of his nose. He fell forward with sodden impact, raising dust.

She stood looking down at him, her breast heaving. A primitive joy danced wildly in her eyes.

Two men shuffled toward her, looking disconcerted, uneasy. She ignored them. She turned to Jose, who was watching from the runway of the barn at the end of the corral fence.

“Bring the horse,” she commanded.

He nodded and disappeared inside. He came out almost immediately, leading a magnificent animal. Temper was a show horse, a pure-bred Arabian of soft golden color; he was her own personal mount.

He snorted and shied away as he saw her. . . . He hung back on the reins as Jose led him to her.

She handed Jose her gun, glanced at Williams’ body. “Get rid of him!” she said contemptuously.

She looked at the big stud. “I want a ride,” she said, “the kind of ride you can give me, Temper!”

Jose’s lips twitched. He watched her stride past him, go into the barn, reappear with big cruel Mexican spurs attached to her half-boots.

He avoided looking at the scar welts on the big stud's flanks.

Some day he'll kill her, he thought.

He held the stallion, talking soothingly and hating himself for the deception. She stepped up into the saddle, settled herself.

Jose stepped back.

She dug the cruel spurs into Temper's flanks and the animal reared up, shrilling in pain. The quirt stung him. He lunged ahead, and Nina Telfors clung to her saddle and laughed, and her laughter was thin and wild and had no joy in it. . . .

Charley Mizner drove into the Diamond T yard an hour after they had buried Sluice Williams. He received the news with outward calm.

"Which way did she ride?" His tone seemed merely curious.

Jock Austin, a rawboned, red-necked, surly man, answered, "Headed for the Tombstones." He took several steps after Charley as the Diamond T manager turned toward the house.

"Moose was due in this afternoon," he reminded Mizner. "Al rode up to relieve him last night."

Charley stopped and looked back, and Jock added: "Bowie thought he'd better check. He rode up to the Dry Creek line house—"

Charley frowned. "If he isn't back by night, take three men and ride after him."

"You expecting trouble?"

Charley nodded. "Baxter's finally backing his loud talk. He's hired four gunslingers. From what I hear, they're tough." He made a motion with his heavy shoulders. "I don't know what move he plans. But it looks like you and the boys are going to have to earn your money for a change."

Jock spat into the dirt. "Four? We'll handle them." He plucked at his ear, frowning. "What about that hombre who fast-gunned Sam?"

"He's staying. Hired on at Rainbow." Charley's eyes held a deep anger.

"Bowie'll be glad to hear it," Jock said. "He ain't been sleepin' good since Sam was killed."

Charley smiled. "He'll get his chance at Winters, real soon." He turned and went into the house, moving with deliberate speed. While Lord Telfors was alive he had occupied the small guest room next to the stairs. After his death Charley had moved into Telfors' room. He had moved in with the confident assurance that he would not be questioned.

Now he went up and changed from his town clothes to riding breeches and a blue flannel shirt and came back downstairs.

Jose was holding a saddled black horse for him in the yard. He mounted with the stiffness of a man who disliked that kind of riding. Jock watched him leave with grudging respect in his gaze.

Charley Mizner was an Easterner and he rode poorly, but he rodded the spread with a firm hand. Somehow none of the gun-quick hands who took his orders ever crossed him.

Charley knew where to look for Nina Telfors. There was little about this girl he didn't know, having made a study of her, as he had of her father, from the day he had come to work for Diamond T. Nina was as wild and unpredictable as the wind, but in some things she deviated as little as the hands of a good watch.

Where the Tombstones tongued into Concho Valley there was a natural amphitheater, surrounded by brooding gray walls and attended by beady-eyed gila monsters, horned toads and slow-wheeling desert hawks.

Charley rode through the narrow defile which led into this amphitheater, and just before he reached it he stopped. He listened above his animal's heavy breathing, heard a horse blow wearily and smiled with chill amusement, knowing that the worst was over.

He dismounted and took the buggy whip he had brought with him and walked through the narrow rocky pass into the wide clearing.

Temper, the big golden stallion, was standing in the middle of the arena, his legs quivering from sheer exhaustion. His proud head was down between his forelegs. He was tied to a mesquite clump, and blood dyed his spur-ribboned flanks.

Nina was lying on her back some twenty feet away, one hand thrown across her face to shield her eyes from the sun.

Watching her, Charley's face was indifferent. He was not a man to be attracted by this girl; there was no substance to her except moody wilfulness and a quick-flaring temper.

The woman at Rainbow was more his kind. He had looked at her the day Luke Snow had brought her to Concho Valley, and he had known then that some day he would win Louella Snow. He had laid his plans to that end, and he was a patient man. He would take over the Diamond T first, then make his move to win Luke Snow's widow.

Nina heard him when he was less than ten feet away. She sat up quickly, fear brightening her sleep-dulled eyes.

He stood over her, a big, patient-seeming man with a whip stock in his hand.

"I thought I told you to stay at the ranch," he reminded her. His voice held no politeness, no respect.

Her eyes grew small and dark, like those of a threatened animal. She started to get up slowly, her body tensed. . . . The whip curled down across her back and she rolled violently, a shriek of pain and anger and hurt pride shrilling from her.

"Williams was obeying my orders!" he said harshly. "I told him to keep you on the ranch."

She cowered, afraid of this man, of his patient cruelty. "He laid hands on me!" she cried. "He hurt me—"

"So he touched you!" Charley mocked. "Williams was no ladies' man. But was his touch worse than the touch of that sniveling Farley? And what would nervous Horace think, if he knew he was kowtowing to a half-breed?"

"No, no!" She put her hands to her face while his cold, measured words whipped her, shredded her pride, bled her more cruelly than the lashing of any whip.

"Next time," he finished, "when I tell you to stay on at the ranch, you stay!"

He wheeled and walked over to the spent stallion, touched its bloody flank. His eyes held an icy fury.

"Near killed him, didn't you? Took your bad temper out on a dumb animal! This horse is worth more than you'll ever be!" He walked back to her, and she covered her face with her hands. "Next time you treat Temper or any other horse like this, I'll use this whip so that the scars will stay with you the rest of your life!"

She kept her hands over her face and cried, deep, wrenching sobs of fear and futility.

His tone was relentless. "He's too spent to carry

you now. Give him an hour more; then ride him back. I'll be waiting for you!"

Without another word he turned and left her. . . .

CHAPTER XII

Lou Winters might have missed that amphitheater. Swinging wide, away from Farley's place, and heading up along the Quicksilver, he saw Charley Mizner ride out of the defile. He swung quickly aside and eased the gray mare among piles of broken shale and dismounted. Reaching in his saddle bag, he brought out a pair of Army binoculars.

Charley's heavy shoulders and head came through the lens. The Diamond T ramrod was pushing a buggy whip more securely into the saddle scabbard which carried a high-powered rifle.

Lou studied the side of the man's face. There was a look of cold satisfaction about Charley, and Lou wondered what the man had been up to. His curiosity piqued, Winters waited until the Diamond T foreman was out of sight, then mounted and rode for the break in the hills.

Riding slowly through the defile, he heard a horse snort up ahead and dismounted quickly, his Colt sliding into his left hand. Alert and wary, he led the mare until he broke out into the clearing.

There was only a girl in the middle of this lost and silent arena. She was on her knees, her face in her hands. He could hear her crying, and he knew she didn't expect anyone to be listening.

The big golden stallion was shaking his head. Blood was drying along the spur cuts. Lou tried to find an answer to this strange scene.

Charley Mizner had obviously met this girl here, and had left. But who had spurred that magnificent animal so cruelly, and on whom Charley had used the whip he couldn't guess.

He holstered his Colt and rolled a cigaret, feeling somewhat uncomfortable, like an intruder on a private scene. He was about to slip away when the stallion saw the mare; a shrill call whistled from him.

The girl froze. Her back went rigid; her hands fell to her sides. When she turned it was with an abrupt gesture, and Lou saw the fear in her face.

He crumbled the unsmoked cigaret between his fingers and let it drop. Fear dissipated slowly in her, and despite the tear stains, he saw that she was remarkably beautiful, and too well dressed for just an ordinary ranch girl.

She looked at him, her eyes widening. Apprehension replaced her fear as he walked toward the big stallion, who turned and eyed Lou with nervous suspicion. When Winters was close the stallion swung around and let fly with his hind feet.

Lou stepped back, shaking his head. He turned to the girl.

"Skittish, ain't he?" His tone was hard.

"Reckon any cayuse would be, after being treated like that."

Nina said nothing. She was still on her knees, and apprehension was still with her.

He said coldly: "Did Charley Mizner do that?"

Nina got to her feet. Her body was still tensed, poised as if to run.

"You know Charley?"

"We've met," he replied. "We're not friends."

"Who are you?"

"Lou Winters." He looked around the empty, darkening arena. "I saw Charley ride out of here. I was curious as to what he was doing—"

"You were spying on us!" Nina Telfors' anger was immediate. She had been crying a few moments before; now she was in a rage. "You dared to spy on Diamond T!"

Lou considered this. Realization came, and with it a sudden cold anger; he looked her over with cool interest.

"So you're Nina Telfors?"

"You've heard of me?" Her voice was quick, feline in its arrogance.

"Little of it good," he replied.

Her face distorted angrily. "Who are you to judge me?"

He grinned. "It might help if I told you Frank Santree was my partner." He waited, but Nina gave no indication of knowing what he meant. He added grimly: "Frank was hanged with Luke

Snow; hanged by Diamond T—on your orders!"

She recoiled. "I gave no such orders!" she cried. "I know nothing of a man named Frank Santree. But Luke—Luke was a thief. He used to work for me. But all the time he was a member of the Doolin band—"

He walked up to her, shaking his head.

"Luke disobeyed me!" she insisted arrogantly. All her posture exuded righteousness now—an arrogance that never questioned itself. She was a savage obeying the impulses of the moment—a creature of few restraints.

"He stole from me! He deserved to die!"

"You are the judge," he murmured.

"This is my land," she flung at him, "all of it. And the people here are my people. I command—and they obey! Or else they suffer the consequences!"

"Princess Nina," he mocked harshly. "Does Charley Mizner obey? Or does he make you obey—with a whip?"

Her reaction was immediate. She whirled and picked up a rock and swung at his face. He caught her arm, and she kicked at his groin; he twisted and caught her knee on his thigh. Her left hand clawed at his face. A long nail ripped the skin across the healing cut made by Bowie's bullet. He caught her other wrist and held her, his own anger rough and hurting.

Behind them the stallion, enraged by the sight

of them struggling, lunged wildly at his picket reins. His strength had returned, and he was a big animal; the reins tore loose from the mesquite bush.

"Kill him, Temper! Kill him!"

Lou flung the girl away. He twisted barely in time to escape the flashing hoofs of the big stud; his gun came smoothly into his palm, by reflex, and he fired twice into the sand under the palomino's belly.

The heavy reports frightened the stallion. He whirled away, found the opening in the arena and disappeared.

The rock hit Lou just above his right ear as he started to turn. The impact sent him to his knees; lights flashed in his head. He tried to get up, stumbled and went down to one knee, his eyes blurred. He had an impression of the girl coming at him, and instinctively he raised his gun.

She shied off. He heard the gray mare snort, mince about. A warning shot through his fogged mind. He shoved himself to his feet and turned, stumbling again, fighting the weakness in his knees. He saw the girl aboard the gray just as she rode through the defile. He had time for one clean shot at her, and he almost took it; sanity came to him just in time.

He brought his hand down, a bleak, wry humor twisting his lips. He took a deep breath and touched the lump over his ear. Then he walked to the defile, made his way through it, and came out on the rock-strewn slope.

Nina Telfors was a speck raising dust in the distance. The sun lay low on the hills, and the land had a red and dying cast. . . .

He touched his lump again. Nina Telfors was wild, irresponsible, dangerous. He had the certain knowledge she would have killed him if she could have, and not given it much thought afterward.

And yet he had the feeling that something dark and dismal was driving her—something she dared not think about; something she shied away from.

He knuckled his jaw slowly. He thought of the woman waiting at Rainbow. Louella, too, was locked up within herself. But there was strength in her, and stability. . . .

He felt a kind of pity for Nina Telfors as he turned and headed south for the ranch on the Quicksilver. . . .

Bowie saw the thin column of smoke against the sky, and it prodded him alert as it revived fearful memories of the last Apache raids. . . . He swung his buckskin aside and studied the smoke, placing its source carefully within the area where the Dry Creek line house was located.

He had not run into Moose on his way back to the main ranch, as he would have if Moose had headed directly for Diamond T. Al Riken, Moose's relief, had taken a pack horse and enough supplies to last him a week. Diamond T rotated its men in this fashion at this lonely northern outpost.

The midday heat pressed down over the low hills. The wind came from the north, from the far snow-capped peaks beyond the valley. Bowie shrugged uneasily.

He remounted and rode more slowly, his boyish features wary, his eyes searching each draw, each clump of rocks. He rode for more than half an hour, and now the smoke column hung in the sky like a blurred exclamation mark, and he knew it came from the line house.

Bowie was too experienced a hand to ride into something he didn't know. There was no reason for that kind of fire . . . no reason at all . . . unless Moose and Al had run into trouble.

It could be a raiding party, but he had not heard of any recent outbreak from the Apache reservation. Still, a man never knew when those red devils would break loose again.

He felt like turning around and heading back to the ranch. But curiosity drew him on. He had to know what had happened to Moose and Al before he went back.

He tied his cayuse to a sapling in a wooded draw and went the rest of the way afoot. He came to the Dry Creek line house from behind, crawling to the edge of a small draw that fed back from the old creek bed.

He stared with bright, hard wonder at the scene below. . . .

The two Diamond T men swung gently from the oak branch. The limb was not high above the ground, and their boots almost scraped the earth. . . . A breeze moved them slowly, turning them so that he had a look at their distorted features.

There was no sign of life around. A timber crackled in the blaze and a shower of sparks went up. But there was no other sound.

Bowie straightened, his rifle held ready across his waist, and walked slowly to the burning line shack. The roof had already fallen in and the sides were ready to collapse. He turned back to the swinging bodies. Both men had been shot, but they had not been dead when they were hanged. His jaw tightened and his stomach churned; he swallowed hard and turned away, forcing himself to study the hard-packed ground for sign.

He was not a good tracker, but he could tell that at least half a dozen men had surprised Moose and Al here. They had come from the south, and they had left heading north. The shoes of their animals were shod, which lessened the probability of an Apache raiding party. He had a feeling that Apaches would have mutilated the bodies as they swung. . . .

If not Apaches, then who?

He couldn't imagine who else would be bold enough to raid Diamond T. Will Baxter had made a lot of threats, but Bowie didn't believe he had the nerve. Besides, this raid had involved at least half a dozen men. . . .

Puzzled and uneasy, Bowie swung around. He trotted to where he had left his horse, suddenly anxious to get back. Charley Mizner would have to be told what had happened here.

He rode at a hard pace, keeping off the skyline and seeking the washes and wooded draws. Sunset caught him skirting the Tombstones, coming down off the long talus slopes toward the free run of rolling range near the Diamond T.

He felt the buckskin tremble and snort tiredly, and he pulled up to give the animal a breather. The shadows were long across the slopes. He slackened in the saddle, his long body relaxing for the first time since he had left the burning line house.

The shock of seeing Moose and Al Riken dangling was still with him. He fashioned a cigaret with unsteady fingers and cupped a match to it. His nerves were jumpy.

It was getting dark fast. He shivered slightly. "Let's go," he muttered to the tired animal, and raked his spurs across the horse's flank.

He cut away from the base of the limestone cliffs and headed down toward the flatland. A line of broken shale, crumbled by some upheaval in the distant past, made a barrier below, slowing his progress.

He was cutting between two dark mounds when a rangy figure stepped out in front of him.

Bowie reacted instantly. He yanked back on the reins, his hand streaking to his holstered gun.

The rangy figure yelled: "Wait—" and twisted violently as Bowie's gun flared. Bowie shot again, cursing the rearing buckskin. The animal twisted like a pretzel to get away from the figure ahead, and a cinch strap popped. The saddle slipped to the right and Bowie fell, kicking free of his stirrups at the last moment.

He landed heavily on his side and lay there, shaken and breathless, fighting the pain in his shoulder and the panic in his brain.

He heard a voice say: "No need to get jumpy, feller. All I want is a lift—"

Bowie recognized that voice as belonging to the man who had killed Sam Keeler. He rolled over and lunged erect, spinning to face the man coming toward him. He fired and saw the rangy man stagger, and desperation jerked his trigger finger. He fired twice more, wildly, and the answering gout of flame spun him around. He opened his mouth wide in a vain effort to suck in air; he didn't feel the other slug which dropped him face down in the loose shale.

Lou Winters leaned against a rock, his teeth

bringing blood to his lower lip. Fire was spreading down his arm and across the muscles of his back. He sucked in a gulp of air and eased his Colt back into its holster.

His right arm felt lifeless. He reached up and probed for the wound with the fingers of his left hand, and found an ugly hole just below his collar bone. He pressed his fingers to the sticky wound and felt the blood pulse against them.

"Darn fool!" he muttered. "All I wanted was a lift."

He walked over to the dark, huddled shape, found a wood match in his pocket and scratched it across a rock. The red flare showed him Bowie's partially turned face . . . he recognized him instantly as the man in Tom's Bar.

The match burned out and he let it fall. He began to laugh, but the laughter was shaken. No wonder Bowie had cut down on him.

He leaned against the nearest mound of shale. He could feel the blood oozing down his side and back, and he guessed that the bullet had gone clean through. He had to get back to Rainbow before he bled to death.

The buckskin had panicked. It might still be running for Diamond T, or it might have stopped somewhere, hampered by the dragging Texas saddle.

Lou forced himself to his feet. The faint clop of a walking horse made him stand still. He waited, hoping, and after what seemed an eternity he saw the buckskin loom up, the saddle dangling, held under the animal's belly by the other cinch strap.

He came forward slowly, as though searching for the man who had been riding him. Lou thanked the gods that be that the buckskin had this sort of attachment to his master. Probably Bowie's personal mount, he thought. A Diamond T animal would have kept heading for home.

He waited until the buckskin came up and nudged the dead man. Then he moved slowly, his voice gentle, soothing. "Easy, boy—no more gunshots." He caught the trailing reins. The buckskin quivered, but made no real effort to break away.

Lou worked around to his side. He unloosened the cinch strap and let Bowie's saddle fall to the ground. He leaned against the animal then, fighting the weakness in his knees.

He couldn't get aboard the animal this way. He led the buckskin to a small outcrop of shale, and from its top he stepped astride the cayuse. His knees tightened against the animal's sides; his left fingers clenched the reins.

"Rainbow," he muttered. "That's where we're headed, fella. . . ."

CHAPTER XIII

Pete knocked the ashes from his corncob, lifted his lanky frame from the short bench in front of the shed and stared into the darkness rimming the trail beyond the Quicksilver. He saw a shadow break the pattern of lamplight from the house, and then a door closed softly and he knew that for the seventh time Louella Snow had come to the porch to look for Lou Winters.

He felt her presence in the darkness across the yard, but he said nothing. Lou was a stranger who had come to Rainbow at noon, asked a few questions, made himself at home, and then ridden off. What did he or Louella Snow know of this man? For all anyone knew, Lou could be a Doolin longrider. Or he could have decided that there was no future here for him, and ridden away.

This last was highly improbable. His roan was still in the corral, and it was a better animal than the gray. And his warbag was up in the loft; Pete had checked to make sure.

He walked back to the bench, his pipe glowing in the darkness. He felt its bite, hot and dry on his tongue, and he realized he had little tobacco left in the bowl. He spat into the night and knocked the rest of the tobacco from the pipe against his heel.

Suddenly restless, he walked over to the porch where Louella's shadowy figure was pressed against the railing.

"Need wood for the stove, ma'am?"

She moved slightly, and he saw her head shake. "There's enough in the wood box, Pete."

He hesitated. "Think he quit?" he asked finally.

She was silent for a long interval. "I don't know. I don't think so."

He shifted uneasily. "He could have run into trouble out there. Anything might have happened."

There was no response from the woman. Finally he shrugged. "Reckon I'll turn in, ma'am," he said, and shuffled away.

Louella kept looking into the darkness. She had a strange, unsettling feeling she could not pin down. She had known this man so briefly. He was a rangy, unsmiling man, harder than Luke, more practical; a man with strength—a self-sufficient man such as Luke had never been. Shame burned in her at the involuntary comparison; she felt disloyal and small.

Yet she could not shake off the appeal of this man she had hired. He was big and capable, and deep within her she felt a need, a feeling she suppressed with angry guilt. She had never loved Luke Snow, but she owed his memory a more enduring respect. . . .

She saw the light burn briefly in the darkness

of the shed, and then after a few moments it went out. She wondered if Pete was asleep. She felt alone and suddenly very tired. She had not relaxed since the morning Luke and Frank Santree had been dropped before the door. . . . The cold numbness was loosening in her now, like a thaw, and she felt afraid and alone and the future held no security.

Not even the hate she felt for Nina Telfors had the capacity to keep this moodiness from her.

She turned and went back into the house and sank into the chair by the table lamp. The coffee pot on the stove sent tendrils of its aroma even here; she had made the coffee fresh against Lou's return.

Every man she had ever known had liked coffee after a hard day's riding. . . .

She picked up the book she had been reading: Charles Dickens' *Tale of Two Cities*. It had been a favorite of Luke's. She stared at the printed pages, but her thoughts were not with Sidney Carton's magnificent sacrifice. She suddenly felt a need for Luke and his comforting presence, and grief came now, silently, and she closed her eyes against the deep sharp pain of the inevitable.

How long she slept she didn't remember. The lamp was still burning when she wakened. . . . The faint clopping of hoofs had roused her, reaching through her sleep.

She started up from her chair. Then she heard

Pete's voice call harshly: "Stand still, fella! I got a gun on yuh—"

She crossed the room, her neck stiff from the position in which she had fallen asleep, her legs prickly from returning circulation.

Lou's voice, strangely weak, sounded from the porch. "It's me, Pete. Winters! I ran into some trouble—"

She flung the door open. He was leaning against the porch support, facing the yard. The lamplight splashed across the boards and diffused upward, showing her his bloodstained jacket and the pallor in his face. His eyes looked big and dark against his drawn face.

Pete came across the yard, a six-gun in his hand. He was in his underwear; he had not bothered to dress. His bare feet padded on the hard ground. He stopped just outside the lamp glow.

A buckskin horse, trailing reins but no saddle, stood by the corral, lapping thirstily at water in the trough.

Lou faced her. "Met Nina Telfors," he said. His teeth showed in a quick smile. "No lady, Louella . . . no lady at all."

His legs buckled then; he hooked an arm around the support and held himself up, breathing hard.

Louella moved to him, slid an arm around his waist. "Pete! Come help me!"

Together they walked Winters into the house, to Louella's bedroom. They laid him on the bed. His eyes flickered and he licked his lips.

"Didn't think I'd make it back." His voice was a whisper. "Not hurt bad—just lost a lot of blood . . ."

She nodded. "Don't talk. Rest. We'll take care of it."

He relaxed. "Wrong about Doolin," he muttered tiredly. "He's in the hills somewhere. Going to be trouble, lots of it. . . ."

He closed his eyes. She turned to Pete. "Go put on a pair of pants," she said bluntly. "I'm going to need your help—"

Morning poked fingers of light across the Quicksilver. The Rainbow rooster strutted out of the barn, beat his chest with his wings, and eyed the black-striped tomcat which came prowling by the corral gate.

The cat froze at the faint sound by the creek. Then he crossed the yard in three jumps and turned the corner. The rooster cocked his head belligerently and eyed the men who rode slowly into the yard.

Pete stirred and turned over on his straw mattress and brushed at something that tickled his nose. It jabbed back at him with painful reproof, and his eyes snapped open.

It took him a few seconds to realize he was looking into the round, dark muzzle of a .45. His eyes shifted to the man holding it, an unshaven, thin-lipped character with a cast in his left blue eye.

The hombre said: “Rise an’ shine, pop. We want yuh outside—”

In the ranchhouse Louella woke with a stiffness in her neck and back muscles. She threw back the blanket and sat upright on the lumpy sofa. Then, remembering the wounded man in the bedroom, she got up quickly and walked to the pump at the sink.

She washed and combed her hair and tied it back in a neat bun on her neck. Then she started the fire in the stove and set last night’s untouched coffee to warm.

The voice at her back was cheerful enough.

“Morning, ma’am.”

She was still too sleepy for her mind to function well. She turned, wondering if Lou had managed to get out of bed without her knowing.

The man in the breezeway door was not Lou. He had Lou’s build, rangy and long-muscled—but his hair was light, and he was dressed neatly, and a thick brown mustache softened the hook of a hawk nose.

She pressed back against the sink, her eyes widening, shock driving the last vestiges of sleepiness from her. The stranger came into the kitchen with a long stride, smiling gently.

He took his hat from his head, bowed slightly. “I’m Doolin, Mrs. Snow.” His eyes were blue, but they had a quicksilver glint, and the gun at his hip held a deadly meaning. "I heard about them hanging your husband, ma'am, and Frank Santree." He wagged his head, but there was no real sadness in his tone. "Poor Frank. He's probably turning over in his grave right now—"

"Herb!"

Doolin stopped. His shoulders tightened imperceptibly, but he kept his easy smile as he turned.

Lou was at the door. Winters' upper body was bare save for the bandage swathing his right shoulder; the gun in his left hand was rock steady.

"Heard you were looking for me," Doolin said pleasantly, ignoring Lou's gun. "Thought I'd drop by and say hello."

Lou's eyes were cold. "It's been a long time between hellos, Herb. Too long." He made a motion with his gun. "Unbuckle your gun belt and let it fall, easy. Then walk this way—"

Doolin laughed. "Still the same Lou Winters. No humor."

"I'm laughing right now," Lou said, and cocked the hammer of his Colt back.

Doolin's smile thinned. "Tell him, Gip," he sneered.

The voice behind Lou was cold and nasal. "Be a good boy, Lou. Put that gun away!"

Lou stiffened. He saw Louella's eyes confirm the threat behind him.

"Herb," he said grimly, "all I have to do is let this hammer fall—"

"You might get me," Doolin agreed bleakly. "But Gip would get you and the girl a second later!"

He saw uncertainty flicker across Lou's eyes, and his smile came back. He walked toward Lou. "Forget it, Winters," he said. His voice held a mock friendliness. "You're outgunned. The rest of my boys are waiting outside."

Slowly Lou eased the hammer down. He jammed the Colt in holster, let out a harsh breath.

Behind him Gip raised his voice. "Come on in, boys! We're eating in style this morning!"

Lou walked into the kitchen, moving to Louella's side. He heard boots tramp through the breezeway, and Pete appeared at the head of a half-dozen hardcases. The man behind him gave him a final shove and guffawed as Pete sprawled over the kitchen table.

Lou said evenly: "What do you want, Herb? What brought you here?"

"Call me Doolin," the outlaw said. "Ace Doolin." He laughed again; he was a man who had always laughed easily. He and Frank had had this in common.

"Herb Dolan died in the war," he added. His voice held a bitterness that was at odds with his character. "Down by that old farmhouse behind Point South Ridge." Laughter came into his eyes again. “That was when Herb figured out the percentages, Lou. No profit in being a hero.”

Lou studied the man. The attack across Point South Ridge was the last he and Frank had seen of Herb Dolan. The war had ended three weeks later. . . .

He remembered the item he had carried for more than a year; the small package he had left with Kathy Hastings at the Palms Hotel.

“You haven’t answered, Ace,” he said. “I thought you were hiding out in Mexico.”

Ace chuckled. “I got tired of *frijoles* and *señoritas*. And we ran out of money.” He saw Lou raise an eyebrow, and he hunched his shoulders. “*Señoritas* cost money, Lou—even in Mexico. Or wouldn’t you know?”

Louella had been looking at them, her face like stone. Now she said: “You want breakfast?”

Doolin bowed. “If you would be so gracious, ma’am.”

Louella turned her back on him and added wood to the fire. Then she walked to the cupboard, took down a small earthen crock, shook her head. “Three eggs.” She turned to Pete, standing like a ruffled rooster by the table.

“I’ll need at least a dozen more, Pete, and a slab of side bacon—”

Doolin said: “Red, go with him. Give the old boy a hand.”

He thought this was funny and so did his men, who broke out into rude laughter.

Pete's neck was red as he walked out, paced by a runty redheaded killer.

"Still packing that U.S. deputy marshal's badge, Lou?" Doolin's voice was casual.

Lou shook his head. "This one was on me, Doolin." His jaw was tight and his eyes held thin cold lights.

Ace frowned. "Quit?"

"Resigned. Right after that Platte City bank holdup you pulled." Lou's voice was level. "I didn't want the government mixed up in my troubles when I crossed the Mexican border after you."

Doolin seemed puzzled. "Why, Lou? What made it personal?"

"My sister."

Doolin's smile faded. He took the pot off the stove and poured himself a cup of coffee.

"I don't get you, Lou. . . ."

"The cashier you killed in that Platte City bank," Lou answered grimly, "was my sister, Herb!"

Doolin shook his head. He glanced at Jake Savage, then back to Lou. His voice held little regret. "She made a run for it, Lou. She should have stayed put—"

Jake was sloshing coffee around in his mug, trying to cool it. "Aw, tell him, Ace. I killed her! All I wanted was a little—"

"Shut up!" Doolin's voice was soft, but it held a deadly menace. Jake became sullen.

But Lou understood. He looked Jake over, fixing the squat, burly man in his mind.

Doolin murmured, "Don't try it, Lou. . . ." His hand came up now, and the Remington was in it, muzzling Winters. "Take his gun," he told one of his men.

It was too late to stop them, Lou thought bitterly. He stood still as one of the outlaws took his gun and tossed it to Doolin, who thrust it carelessly in his waistband.

"We'll hide out here for a day or two." Doolin chuckled. "Better than sleeping out in the hills."

He refilled his coffee cup. "Ought to thank me, ma'am," he told Louella. "Gip told me about Diamond T hanging your husband and Frank Santree." He chuckled again. "We thought we'd help out—give them a little of their own medicine. We left a couple of them swinging up in their north line house—"

Lou started. So that was where Bowie had been. He'd probably been on his way back to Diamond T with the news when Lou ran into him.

Charley Mizner would not take it without hitting back. But hitting back at whom?

"Diamond T's been claiming you've been raiding them," Lou put in as a feeler. "They'll be looking for you—"

"Not for me," Doolin replied. "Don't know

what this Diamond T ramrod's up to, but he won't be looking for me. He knows we're not in the hills. Looks like he's been stealing his own spread blind, and using me and my boys as goats. I thought we'd give him something to remember us by."

Lou licked his lips. "Why stay here?"

"Just for a day or two," Doolin said. His eyes narrowed. "You'll be riding with us when we leave. Gip here was in town long enough to get a line on the bank. We'll bust it wide open on our way back south—and sometime during the fracas some townsman's lucky shot is going to kill you, Lou. . . ."

Louella turned from the stove, her face white. Doolin caught the expression on her face, and his eyes narrowed.

"Well, I'll be goldarned," he muttered softly, and began to chuckle again.

CHAPTER XIV

Jock Austin and three Diamond T men found Moose and Al Riken still swinging. The line shack had burned to the ground.

He looked for Bowie, but found no sign of the man. Jock had no idea who had raided this line house, or why, or what had happened to Bowie.

They packed Al and Moose on one cayuse, and the rider rode double with Jock back to the ranch.

Charley Mizner met them in the yard. Jock's explanation was brief and to the point.

"About six, seven men, near as I can make out, came down on the line house. Moose and Al didn't have a chance."

Charley took out a cigar. "Bury them with Sam and Williams," he ordered. "Then come back and saddle fresh horses. Saddle the black for me. We're riding into town."

Jock's voice held surprise. "Baxter?"

"Who else?"

Jock frowned. "I didn't think he had the nerve—"

"Hired guns can give a man courage," Charley said. "He's got four guns behind him now—maybe more. Tomorrow we might be outnumbered—"

Jock grinned with sudden understanding. "Hit him now and get him out of the way, eh?"

"He's been making threats against Diamond T," Charley said calmly. "All of Concho has heard them. Who will blame us if we ride into town and call him on it?"

Jock nodded. Then, remembering the man who had killed Sam, he asked: "What about that hombre who claimed he was Frank Santree's partner?"

Charley smiled. "Heard he hired out to Rainbow. We'll pay that spread a visit, after we take care of Baxter." He sucked in smoke, his eyes like pale glass. "Frank Santree was his partner—and Frank was caught red-handed rustling Diamond T beef. Winters could wind up the same way—"

Jock shrugged. "Wish Bowie was here. The darn fool might have gone looking for Winters—"

Charley watched him take charge of the bodies. There were eight men at the ranch on whom he could count. Most of them had been handpicked by him over the years. He had been mighty careful. Telfors was a hard man to fool. But he had managed to talk Telfors into getting rid of Baxter, and then Telfors' own unforeseen death had opened the way to gaining control of Diamond T for himself.

In the beginning he had been content to steal Diamond T beef, use the outlaw Doolin as a cover. In that respect it had not been too hard to fool Telfors; the man was still green about the country. There were others in the valley who were more skeptical—but none of them had any love for Lord Telfors, known bitterly by many as “High and Mighty Telfors.” If they suspected what Charley Mizner was up to, none of them cared to tell Telfors.

Except Luke Snow.

Charley had wondered about Luke. He had ridden for Diamond T for years, a quiet, introspective man with the odd habit of sticking his nose in a book when he wasn’t working. Telfors hadn’t liked him, but had respected him. Neither Telfors nor his daughter had liked it when Luke had come back from a trail drive with a wife. . . .

Charley turned and looked up at Nina’s window. He saw the drapes move and knew she was watching. He took the cigar from his mouth and rolled it between his fingers.

There was no more profit in waiting. He would have been content with the money he had gained from Diamond T beef, but now only this girl stood between him and all of it.

He walked to the house and looked up the broad curving flight of stairs before mounting them. He heard the kitchen door open, but didn’t bother to see who it was.

He didn’t knock.

Nina was by the vanity, running her hands

through her loose hair, when he entered. She didn't look at him.

He said: "I'm going to town. We're going to take care of Baxter."

She kept ruffling her hair, smiling at herself in the mirror. She was like a little girl refusing to listen to her father.

"I'm leaving a man behind," he said. "Don't try to leave. He won't be as careless as Sluice Williams."

He took a legal document out of his coat pocket and walked to her, laying it down on the vanity. "I picked this up in town yesterday. It's a bill of sale for Diamond T. I want you to sign it."

She turned, her face wild.

"I won't sign it! You can't make me!"

He smiled. "I'm offering you freedom," he said. "It's more than you deserve. I'm giving you ten thousand dollars, and a ticket to New Orleans. You ought to make out fine there. Your kind does—"

Her hands clawed. But fear restrained her. This man was the only man who struck terror in her.

"I won't sell for that," she cried. "Dad put more than six times that much money in this ranch—"

"That was before Doolin," Charley said. "Diamond T doesn't have a third of the beef it once grazed."

She licked her lips. "There is no Ace Doolin,"

she whispered. "There never has been. Father was getting suspicious about it. If he had lived, you'd never have gotten away with it." She tossed her head angrily. "I won't sign it! And you can't keep me captive here forever. Some day I'll get away—"

"You'll sign," he said grimly, "or I'll see that everyone in the valley knows about you, even your friends at the capital."

She shrank from him as though he had struck her.

"Who would listen to you?" he sneered. "A half-breed, someone Lord Telfors—"

She whirled, put her hands to her ears. He pushed the bill of sale toward her.

"I'll expect to find it signed when I get back. I'll pick up tickets for you and Juanita on the Saturday stage out of Concho. . . ."

She didn't answer. Even after the door closed behind him she made no move. . . .

They came into Concho by Ward's Hay & Feed Store. Charley Mizner shifted his sore rump and waited with the others while Jock Austin dismounted and cut across the alley to Main Street.

He was gone less than twelve minutes.

"They're in front of GOPHER'S STORE," he said shortly. "Four of them. Baxter's with them. They're loading a buckboard with supplies."

Jock grinned. "Looks like they plan to settle somewhere."

Charley nodded. "We'll give them a homestead," he said dryly. "Up on Boot Hill!"

"They're not pushovers," Jock added thoughtfully. "We'd better play this with an ace-in-the-hole."

Charley nodded. "Take another man with you—" He waited until Jock and the other rider disappeared in the alley. Then he looked over his remaining riders.

"Let's get it over with!"

Will Baxter was smoking a thin cigar on the store porch, watching the supplies being loaded on the buckboard. There was a glint of satisfaction in his eyes.

Myers was in an ugly mood, which was the way Baxter wanted him. Myers and Gates were going to the Dry Creek line house. The Striker brothers would help them take the place over, unload supplies, and then run down to Copper Springs.

By the time Charley Mizner recovered, Knowles should have sent the rest of the men. . . .

His gaze lifted above the buckboard to the riders who had just turned the corner. Surprise chained him to the store support.

Reb Myers was standing by the wheel, smoking. He had refused to handle the supplies.

His broken nose still pained him and there was a smoky anger in his eyes.

He saw the look that came over Baxter's face, and he whirled to face the mounted men. Gates, a sack of flour on his shoulder, let it fall and stepped back. . . .

Charley Mizner said harshly: "I hear you're going to break Diamond T, Will! Hired four guns to help you!"

Baxter went pale. The sweat stood out brightly against his face. He had not expected this—not a showdown in town. He had underestimated Charley. And now it was too late.

The realization came to him now that his plan had been too simple; that it had seemed workable only to him. He had planned his moves like a bad chess player, not taking into account the possible moves Charley might make against him.

The Striker brothers came out of the store, carrying boxes. They were caught flat-footed.

Myers whirled, snarled: "They've got us cornered, Lee!" and went for his gun.

Jock's rifle, centered on him, doubled Myers up before his gun cleared holster. The sharp crack from the alley across the street was the signal that touched off ten seconds of hell in Concho.

The Striker brothers didn't have a chance. Les didn't even have time to drop the box. Bob Striker tried to get back inside the store and died crossing the threshold!

Gates managed to kill the man next to Charley before he died. Will Baxter stood frozen against the support. Jock's rifle hit him twice. The cigar fell from his mouth, trailing sparks, as his lips slackened. He brushed a hand across his face, as if to clear his dimming vision; then he fell face down across the store steps.

George Asher was in the barbershop when the shooting started. There was still lather on his face when he ran out. He saw the mounted men in front of GOPHER'S STORE, but it took him a few moments to realize what was happening.

He drew his gun, and his first shot spilled a Diamond T man out of saddle. Then Jock, stepping clear of the alley, cut down on him.

The marshal spun around, blood dying the side of his face, mixing with the lather. He was dead before he hit the ground.

The racketing explosions bounced back from the sandstone hills and faded. The mounted men fought fidgety horses.

Charley Mizner glanced up and down the street. He had a rifle in his saddle boot, but he had not even drawn it.

Eight men lay dead in the street. Two of them were Diamond T riders. He waited while his men loaded the two bodies onto riderless horses. Then, in a compact group, they swung away from the general store and headed out of town.

Kathy Hastings came up the street, lead

dragging at her feet. Then she saw George's crumpled figure and darted off the walk, knelt by his body. She screamed, wild, racking screams that tore through the shocked town. . . .

It took twenty minutes for Paul Stockton to organize a posse. Reverend Stone, shocked by the brutal killings, rode with them. They overtook the Diamond T rider Charley had delegated to bring the bodies back to the ranch. Threatened by half a dozen rifle muzzles, the rider readily told them where Charley was headed. . . .

CHAPTER XV

Heat came over the land, the quick heat of October that would dissipate with the evening chill from the high north peaks. Rainbow drowsed in the afternoon sun.

Doolin and his men played poker in the front room. Pete was used as an errand boy, to fetch water, coffee, whatever came to the mind of these men.

Louella sat in a chair and hid her thoughts behind a stony countenance. She used her hands to patch a pair of Luke's old socks; she needed to do something, or her control would break.

Lou read. He had the *Tale of Two Cities* in his hands and he was looking down at the printed pages, but he might as well have been gazing at the moon. He had managed to get a shirt over his bandages. His shoulder throbbed, but a night's rest and breakfast had renewed his strength. He felt restless and cornered, as in fact he was. He knew Doolin meant what he had said.

Whatever friendship had been between him and this man and Frank Santree had vanished in the years after the war.

He lifted his regard to Doolin.

The outlaw boss sat back in his chair, his hat tilted back from his forehead. There was a raffish look about him, but the lines about his mouth were harsh, belying the smile he kept on his lips.

Herb Dolan had found no profit in war—and had found little more in his present career. It wasn't money that really mattered, Lou thought. A man lived by what he made and was content, or he always wanted more. Doolin and his men had taken sixty thousand dollars from the Platte City bank. The money had lasted them little more than four months.

His attention focussed on Jake Savage, a burly, hairy animal of a man with eyes that shone greedily even when he was playing penny ante poker. This was the man who had killed his sister. Lou's stomach knotted at the thought, and his hands clenched with an unconscious show of feeling.

He felt Louella's eyes on him and looked at her. She smiled a little; then her glance went to the card players. They seemed intent on their game, their voices rough and sometimes obscene, ignoring her presence or taking no account of her feelings.

She looked at Lou and inclined her head slightly. He glanced at the sofa. She seemed to have indicated something there, but he didn't know what. He made a slight, puzzled gesture.

Some time later the stringy, balding man Doolin had left out by the creek as a guard came running into the house.

"Bunch of riders!" he said tersely. "Coming from town, seems like—"

Doolin kicked his chair back and got to his feet. A scowl blackened his face. "How many?"

"Six. Naw, seven, with a big jasper in town clothes riding up front."

Doolin's gaze shuttled to Lou. Winters grinned. "Looks like Diamond T's come to smoke you out, Herb!"

Doolin shook his head. "Not me, Lou," he snarled. "They don't know I'm here. They're after you, I reckon." He rubbed the palm of his hand over his Remington, and began to chuckle. "They've been yelling wolf a long time, boys! Let's give them something to howl about!"

He put a hand on the shoulder of the man next to him. "Stay here, Shuster. Keep an eye on Winters and Luke's widow. This won't take long."

Doolin and the rest of his men went out the back way. They took Pete with them. . . .

Shuster, a toothless, stoop-shouldered man still under thirty, drew his Colt. He pulled a chair away from the table and set it near the window. The curtains shielded him from the yard, but he had a good view of the show about to take place.

Louella put down her sewing. She rose, and Shuster swiveled to face her, his gun menacing her. "Sit down, sister," he lisped. "You make me nervous!"

"I want a drink of water," Louella said firmly. She used the pump and drank, then walked back to the sofa. She sat down next to Lou, close to the end of the sofa.

Shuster said: "None of that! Not while I'm here!"

Lou got up. He walked to the sink. "This far enough?"

Shuster relaxed. "Aw, sit down. On the chair there." He wiped his nose with the back of his hand. "Let's listen to the fun."

The silence dragged. The clock ticked steadily, and Lou thought of Charley Mizner riding to his death. He had used Doolin to cover his raids on Diamond T, never thinking Ace Doolin would actually show up. He had cried wolf until the wolf had finally come. . . .

The sound of approaching riders finally seeped into the silence. Shuster tensed, a grin cracking his homely face.

There was a long moment of silence. Then Charley Mizner's deep voice broke the stillness.

"Probably saw us coming and hightailed it, Jock. Take a look in the house—"

The flat report of a .45 cut him off.

Shuster was looking through the window when Louella slid her hand under the sofa pillow for the Colt she kept there. She had put it there the night Luke and Frank Santree had died. . . .

She got it up and around, the muzzle pointing

toward Shuster, just as the outlaw swung his attention back to her.

He was holding his gun in his lap; surprise coursed through him. He jerked then and fired a shot quickly, before he was ready, and Louella's Colt slammed heavily.

Shuster took the bullet in his stomach. He came up out of the chair and fell backward; his weight hit the panes and crashed through.

Lou reached the woman before Shuster's body disappeared. He took the gun from her limp hand. She was slumped forward, a dazed look on her face.

"Did he hit you?" There was sharp concern in his voice.

She shook her head. He hauled her to her feet. Outside, the firing was ragged. Lou had the feeling that Charley and his riders, caught in a crossfire, had not put up much of a fight.

"Get out the back way. You'll have a chance to run for it."

She shook her head. "Rainbow belongs to me. It's my fight, too."

There was no time to argue. The firing had all but ceased outside. Lou went to the door, opened it a crack.

Doolin and Jake were in the yard, just in front of the porch. They were standing over Charley Mizner's body, and Jake was holding the reins of a big black stallion.

Gip Upson and two others were coming around the corner of the shed.

The first rifle shot cracked over Upson's head, splintering wood from the shed. Doolin's head jerked around. Jake's voice came in a thick, surprised snarl. "Thought we got 'em all—"

The posse broke across the creek, spreading out as they rode. Doolin whirled. He came up the steps just as Lou flung the door open and stepped out.

Doolin stopped.

Lou's voice was bitter. "There's no place to go, Herb—" He fired a split-second before Doolin, saw the killer spin around and go slack as he fell. Then he shifted his gun to Jake.

But the burly man managed to get the stallion between them. He broke for the shed, the nearest structure that would offer some cover. . . .

Pete appeared in the doorway. They had forgotten him during the fight. He stood now, the stock of an old 12-gauge shotgun tucked under the stump of his arm.

The blast seemed to cut Jake Savage in two. . . .

The fight quickly sieved out of the others. The posse rounded them up, those who were alive, including those who were wounded.

Paul Stockton listened to Louella's explanation and then to Lou. Winters held out a hand. "Looks like I talked out of turn the other day," he apologized. "I'm glad I was wrong about you."

• • •

Reverend Stone himself brought the news to Diamond T—to Nina Telfors.

She looked out over the darkening range from the high arch of the portico over the front door—to an empire dissolved in blood. She was strangely calm.

"I should have sold Diamond T when my father died," she said. "I don't belong here."

Reverend Stone said nothing to this. In a way she was right. Concho Valley was no place for her kind of woman.

"One of your men, Jock Austin, talked before he died, Miss Telfors. He told the posse how Charley Mizner had used the Doolin gang as an excuse to steal from Diamond T."

"Charley did more," she said coldly. There was no forgiveness in her voice. "He tried to steal Diamond T from me. I'm glad he's dead!"

Reverend Stone shrugged. "He cried wolf—and the wolf came—" He shook his head. "Greed and hate are terrible things, Miss Telfors."

"Thank you, Reverend," she cut him off, "but I'm in no mood for sermons."

The minister nodded stiffly. "As you wish." He touched his hat to her and left.

There was lightness in her step as she turned and went into the house. Maybe Charley Mizner had been right after all. New Orleans was a gay, bright place. And no one there would know she was a sham, a half-breed.

She began to sing as she started to pack. . . .

Lou Winters said goodbye to Louella Snow three days later. His shoulder was healed enough for him to travel. And he had a number of things to settle up north.

But he stopped by the Palms Hotel first, to pick up the package he had left in the hotel safe.

The desk clerk took his receipt and handed the package to him. He was a small nervous man who was taking Kathy Hastings' place. Kathy had collapsed after George Asher's death and had still not recovered enough to work.

Lou took the medal out of the chamois bag; a small bronze medal similar to a thousand others given for honor and bravery above the call of duty on the battlefield.

The War Department had thought Herb Dolan dead at the battle of Point South Ridge—one of many tragic mix-ups of the bloody war—and had sent the medal to Lou after a search had failed to reveal any living relatives of Dolan.

Lou stopped by the cemetery on the hill outside of Concho. The posse had buried Doolin and the others here. Strangely enough, Doolin's grave was next to Frank Santree's.

Lou laid the medal on Herb Dolan's grave and rode on. . . .

Center Point Large Print
600 Brooks Road / PO Box 1
Thorndike, ME 04986-0001 USA

(207) 568-3717

US & Canada:
1 800 929-9108
www.centerpointlargeprint.com